Distance Between Life and Death

Alfric Asiago

First Edition: June 2014
Published by Nsemia Inc. Publishers (www.nsemia.com);
Oakville, Ontario, Canada

Edited By: Sheena Brennan
Cover Concept & Illustration: Alfric Asiago
Cover Design: Danielle Pitt
Layout Design: Kemunto Matunda

Note for Librarians:
A cataloguing record for this book is available from
Library and Archives Canada.

ISBN: 978-1-926906-38-6

Dedication

To Ben Carson Sr., M.D. you made me know that a person who removes a mountain starts with removing stones. You made me know that a great achievement starts with as simple step as identifying an obsidian rock and ends up as complicated as becoming a neurosurgeon.

Disclaimer

To any person identifying himself or herself with characters in this book whether living or dead, places and even thinks is suffering from guilt of doubt and instincts of blame: this is fictitious material.

Foreword

HIV/AIDS in Africa has consistently posed the challenge of communicating behaviour change to vulnerable populations. The need for effective communication requires that we look continually for innovative ways of passing on the message on risks and preventive measures to different types of population and in ways in which the recipients will continue to listen, learn and behave accordingly. Fiction is one such way. Good fiction has to be both educating and entertaining for effective communication to be achieved. For certain if not most populations, learning from fiction is enhanced by the provisions of creative writing which allow the readers to identify with life-like situations and analyze motivations, actions and consequences. This communicative and educative provision of fiction has been used effectively in this story to pass on important lessons to young populations.

The book is a story that engages in the less talked about realities of how HIV/AIDS affects individuals' lives, leading to far reaching consequences that affect an individual in very significant ways. The story is based on how individual reasoning affects our behavior leading to actions engendering the spread of the HIV/AIDS. The story, in a very precise way, attempts to relate cause to effect using appropriate artistic tools. It communicates in practical and relatable ways to the consequences of drug abuse and irresponsible sexual behavior. The story is modulated to not only communicate these but to navigate the reader through different emotions, from joy to sadness, love to hatred and patience to anxiety.

The author adopts a philosophical approach to affect his target audience in a bold and prudent way. His narration seeks to interface fiction with the real world experiences. The author compares and contrasts situations giving different points of view to achieve a focused narration that is however fairly coherent in its central message.

For the reader, it is expected that this story provides experiences that, if well reflected upon, will offer the basis for prudent decision making specifically in relation to sexual behavior and relationships. The book will engage the reader, calling them to analyse situations and make sound decisions rather than surrender to instincts and sensations that could have devastating long term and irreversible consequences. The author has, with admirable sensitivity, sought to communicate to the reader, and put across lasting lessons and has thereby made a significant contribution in addressing the challenges of communication behavior change in the face of the HIV/AIDS pandemic.

Dr. Michael Wainaina
Senior Lecturer
Department of Literature
Kenyatta University

About the Author

Alfric Nyakundi Asiago holds Bsc. in Environmental Science from Kenyatta University, Kenya. He is a model, a footballer and a musician. He has done works of fiction for many years, but none attracted national recognition to the degree of the poems which appeared in poetry corner of the *Moments Magazine* of *The East African Standard* (now *The Standard*) between the years 2005 and 2006. In 2010 and 2011, Alfric participated in competitions of the *National Book Development Council of Kenya* in the category of adult fiction category. He is also multi-lingual, being able to communicate fluently in English, Kiswahili, Portuguese, Japanese and Chinese. His inspiration to work hard and succeed was triggered by reading real stories of Doctor Ben Carson who demonstrated that there can be possibilities even in the face of strongest winds of doubt.

Alfric is currently editor of fiction and opinion columns at *The Companile Magazine* published at Kenyatta University.

Distance Between Life and Death is Alfric's first full-length novel.

Chapter One

Maria Fabiano, the Portuguese professor, would have given a lecture on how it was going to be difficult becoming my lecturer. She kept on shifting her eyes from the female tattoos on my arms to her cell phone on the table, and she would have sworn that I would have stolen it within seconds if she walked out of the office. I saw her thinking fruitlessly by scratching her head and touching her spectacles on the most suitable way she would use to get along with me as she went through my file on her lap.

Her dark brown stockings, which she never took off, fitted her legs tightly and passionately; it was difficult to tell it was not her skin colour unless one looked at her hands or face. She whistled a Portuguese tune as she ran her hand through the neatly arranged papers, which was a masculine thing in many African communities. A couple of times she creased her face and adjusted her spectacles then kept on looking at me as she went through my documents. When she finished she asked me additional details before she returned my file to the shelf.

I was late by one week at Mark's because I was still looking for the most comfortable way I would leave my five-year-old adopted son, Russel, whose mother had died in her late teens. He had seen me punching our houseboy Tom on the nose the day before after he joked that I was stupid to enter fatherhood when life promised young love and money. He went on describing Russel as a weed seedling whose roots should have been denied soil access at the beginning of the planting season. He was lucky his mongrel Clinton broke his chain and came to his rescue. I got over it only after he apologized to me later that day.

"I'm sorry Tom, that did not break your neck too," I told him when I saw how bad his nose was.

He pinched the blood soaked bandage to assess how bad it was and opened his mouth wide toward the sky in pain, like a fingerling in search of air.

"You were lucky you got away Brooks," he said.

"Most preferably I should have gone for your head. It really prevents you from thinking," I told him casually.

He did not know that I was serious.

When I ran out of options I left Russel with my step mother. She had criticized his adoption all along and felt the child should have been taken to a children's home but she did not know that taking care of him was a lifelong promise I made to his mother who had put all her trust in me. I did not tell her all that because I felt it was not necessary to debate about an innocent child who did not even know what was happening. My stepmother was an old fashioned woman who did not believe a young man should take care of a child who was not his own. Although he did not say anything, Russel did not like her either. He preferred to come and watch me work while sucking on his thumb than sit in the kitchen to see her make food. He followed me everywhere the day I left home and seemed to trust a sixth sense which told him I was going away. When I left that day for college he cried hysterically. He only kept quiet, whimpering heavily, when I promised him new shoes.

When Mrs. Fabiano finished making a call she

fished a handout from the pile on the table and pushed it towards me. She then took the trouble of making me a cup of coffee, which was something unusual that we were not used to at that time in the country, where workers in any hierarchy served us with a master-to-servant kind of attitude. She must have done it several times before, and the people she did the courtesy, protested because I saw her prepare lips to counter any refusal. When I accepted the offer in good faith she was surprised but never showed it.

"Thanks," I said.

"Welcome," she said preparing her own.

"Brooks Ishimwe, right?" She asked politely.

"Yes," I replied.

"You are late," she said.

"I'm sorry," I said shrugging and regretted it.

As I began opening the handout to kill time she found more time to look at my hair which was tied into a pony tail. There was that first impression which failed me every time no matter how hard I tried. Almost all the things I liked did not go well with it. I usually remedied it by maintaining a hard face which sent wrong implications of who I really was. I do not recall how many times I was out of offices for allegations of rudeness back in high school, or worse, spent mornings cleaning halls on weekdays because of such kind of false perceptions.

"Copy the timetable from the notice board," she said.

"Portuguese is a nice language, and its culture, like its diversity, is interesting. I promise it will be fun learning it."

I kept quiet not knowing what to promise myself.

Her voice was a little official then. Twelve years in Africa had taught her a thing or two on how to deal with us.

"You will have an opportunity to visit Brazil in your third year as well as experience many Portuguese events and places during the course," she added.

Just then her male secretary, Maina, entered with a file. He left a smell of recent tobacco behind him as he moved. His beltless locally tailored trouser was so over ironed that it was shining at the hems. He placed the file on the table carefully with the usual secretary nervousness brought about by imagined feelings of bad observations in the presence of their bosses, then adjusted it as if it was a baby to meet those tutorials in trainings which insisted on neatness. When he was convinced he stood undecided whether to get out or wait for her directions.

"If you will have questions feel free to ask me. I wish you a nice time at the department of Portuguese," she said and extended her hand.

"Thank you," I said, taking it.

She turned to Maina.

"Go and tell him more about the department."

She looked at her cell phone to confirm it was in its place. Experience coached her not to trust natives who took stealing as a game. I walked out with the handout knowing her eyes were behind me. Maina closed the door silently which, as usual, had a notice to tell whoever was entering to first clear with the secretary. He cleaned his nostrils with the tip of his forefinger as he warmed up for the rare opportunity to exercise the authority of familiarity. The poor man had smoked himself coloured. His thin fingers and eyes were black. As he dragged his slender frame in baggy clothes in which he was widely absent he looked dead by nicotine and the only thing which suggested he was a living thing was movement. When insisting on something he looked like an infuriated wild kitten.

"In this department you have to be obedient to your seniors all the time," he said with a creaking voice.

I was surprised by the unwelcome statement in an institution of such a level. One good or bad thing with me was that I did not take too long to tell how I wanted my things to go.

"What is your name?" he asked shaking from the previous day's hangover.

"Composure is my name," I said, feeling nothing.

"You should also adopt it because it is very fundamental for your kind of job," I finished, then walked away.

I saw him shake his head through the mirror erected on the wall at the end of the corridor.

Mark's University College of Foreign Languages along Thika Road stood on the outskirts of Nairobi, the capital city, which was the focal point of business and socialisation. It was a branch of Mark's University in Lancashire England, which offered language degrees and limited scholarships for the best students in various categories who wished to join. I had secured myself a scholarship after I graduated first in my class from the school of journalism, and I still held an unbeaten record of the best provincial student in high school for the last five years. There were more applications than the college could admit because of its international link. An opinion poll the previous month indicated that locals preferred foreign higher learning institutions over local ones. My father was one such example who looked at the country of origin on anything he bought and he would gladly pay whenever he saw a 'Made in England' tag.

Like any other Monday morning I knew, the offices would be full of commitments with hurrying secretaries and messengers from one office to the other who then went to sit behind computers which clicked to commands and rejected applications as if they had been used ages ago. There was that tendency of forgetting everything and dumping it beyond reach on Fridays when everyone ran away from offices as if it was some sort of a penitentiary. They woke up on Mondays with regrets cursing daybreak with their formatted minds which did not even remember passwords to vital documents but had to stick to the jobs somehow because their lives and those of their ever eating children depended on them. It would have been an insult if one wanted them to remember all unfinished work of the previous week without referring somewhere but they insisted everyday they were for the best interests of the nation.

Having gone through four years at the school of journalism, I was aware that adventure was the order of the day for youngsters in learning institutions. They insisted on weaving relationships which were fueled by excitement away from home and would not believe they would not work until it happened. Mark's was not an exception. Relationships which dominated us under the bracket of those tender years were a solid existence because I saw it right away in smiles and gestures along corridors. It was a majority stage in life which won numbers and anybody who missed it in action then did not miss it in his mind. Within just a week after the commencement of lessons the students looked like they had known each other for a long time. I was the only person who felt like a stranger. Not because I was new but there was something which always pulled me away from collective reasoning. Keeping time was my second problem. No matter how hard I tried there was always something pulling me back. It made me feel different every time. Although I knew it was not something good, I preferred staying alone and look at what other people did.

There were a number of students leaning on pillars along pavements talking with lit faces to pass time or wait for lessons. The girls listened, nodding at intervals to agree or encourage the boys who did the talking. To be honest, there were times I wished that was like them. I have to admit this because as an investigative journalist, I knew it was not a good thing to be distinguished. If they got along well they moved to different places like food shops for refreshments or to nature zones where people were fewer. When the girls became disinterested they would be seen looking at themselves in small pocket mirrors or scrubbing off Cutex from their nails and those talking to them did not need to be told that they were boring. When it was time for lectures or other commitments they exchanged phone numbers and went on their way with promises of seeing each other some other time. Others would come to the same places and the same scenarios would happen. It was an endless activity.

As I walked around to master the most important places, a couple of female eyes flashed towards me. I was not surprised. I knew that they had quickly noted I was new, but I was a different kind of new student altogether. The basis of understanding such simple feminine behavioural science was that they took note of everyone who was new and spent some time to unearth a few more details before they staged up correlations. They would absorb many details within a short time and maintain casual looks as if they knew nothing. For the time I had worked in the field of investigative journalism, they were the people I knew who possessed detailed information. Those within close proximity greeted me with passionate smiles on their faces while boys talking to them looked at me with impatience. Again, that was not strange at all. Girls were always interested in something new and discarded it whenever they saw something else. The only thing one needed to do to stop them from shifting their attention was to maintain their interests by surprising them more than anybody else which was not something easy.

There were a number of new buildings that were being put up in the direction of the largest lecture hall which was an indication that the college was still new. Machines roared in disagreement as men under pressure worked on them incessantly. Asian supervisors in red helmets hovered around with notebooks under their arm pits and pens in their hands warning anybody who slowed down the speed of work. They were chasing deadlines by working day and night with bulbs dangling from temporal posts all over the site. There were strong disagreements as to why contracts were not allocated to locals, but when an advertisement of a railway expansion was put in the newspaper there was not a single local firm that clocked half of the requirements. Quality seemed to be the secret weapon towards winning tenders and that was what kept foreign firms smiling. Locals received casual jobs without question and had to work for long hours with little pay.

A considerable number of movements towards the library, particularly at the beginning of a semester, were not unusual for new students. When I looked towards them, I knew that with time it would vaporize like the morning dew in appearance of sunshine and would resume again on the week of examinations and never to happen at the beginning of semesters except for new students. The only continuing students who would make friends with the library from the beginning to the end were those from poor families. Those we loved to call "book worms" with pathetic looks from cheap clothing, repaired and over-polished shoes as well as specific cheap menus with an economical consistency would be seen frequenting the libraries. To them snack time was a vocabulary. Terrible as it sounds only few excelled while quite a number failed. I had failed to convince my father that standards of living had nothing to do with class work and that it was an individual choice but he strongly believed the rich were likely to fail. Years later, when I read about psychologists who collectively agreed economic standards were a major determinant of class excellence; I did not know what to believe then.

In a higher learning institution like Mark's where students were basking on what they called freedom, one might have asked what made new students go to libraries the first week of the semester. For one there were those lectures parents gave them the night before reporting to school. The talks might have varied but at long last all converged to excelling in class and cautioned against questionable company as well as embracing morality and joining religious organizations. Very few people will disagree that we usually giggled inwardly at the mention of religious issues such as those Christian unions we so much loved to brand hypocrites.

which ones were applicable and which ones were exceptions. There was no one who exempted class excellence from their list, even when it brought a different result some time later. So then going to the libraries when the course outline had been barely read was not a surprise. Therefore it is true to say that almost all the students in the library a few days after opening were new. The older ones spent their time in the newspaper and magazine reading zones.

Then there were those self driven dreams which everyone seemed to embrace so much without desire to let go. A first class would ring in the head from the beginning and of course a beautiful girlfriend here or an understanding boyfriend there. All these images created in our minds were very vital in shaping our future for better or worse. They were fundamental for our self-esteem and the amount we worked or the way we behaved depended on them. Then the cold truth of their application created irreversible changes in the way we perceived things and what we really thought about life. One would realize that it was not only about reading hard. For examinations, you would have to be well prepared. It did not matter how long you waited for the right partner but how much you were willing to adjust some your dreams. I had seen insane theories in relationships when I was in the school of journalism, which they claimed would have made cats lay eggs and turn clay into cake. To stick to the end those promises youngsters gave each other was as difficult as asking people to pay for sunlight.

There were others who thought otherwise; far away from the promises yet so near. I would not have believed a second-hand narration had I not witnessed it with my roommate Meyer 'the player' who interpreted life upside down. A shock to many, he believed it by becoming active in a lifestyle at that time many would have considered suicide. To many it was pure guesswork and mob psychology, while to people like me it was the most mysterious thing I had ever known. I often felt embarrassed admitting to myself that I had no information on the existence of such a person, given that the career I chose constantly needed updated information, like that of a spy. He was the most handsome man I had ever seen yet the most dangerous thing I had ever known, whose secret weapon was soft talk and zero irritation. Being a great narrator with real life experiences flowing out of his lips, milk would have over boiled without noticing when one was listening to him. Anyone who did not know him would have dismissed his allegations as fiction because he did not need to search his memory much to say something which happened years back.

The same evening after my arrival, I found Meyer chatting with a young teenage girl in a full blue school uniform. To date, fear and caution grips me whenever I see such a uniform because it taught her a lesson about ignorance and unlike many people, I was lucky to learn from it. Half consumed cokes and a bag of crisps were on the table where they sat in such a way that there was no distance between them. He introduced her to me as his girlfriend Eve and did not say anything more. He was keen then and chose his word when such visitors were around. She kept on swinging her legs under the table, chewing gum, and she did not show interest or curiosity to know who I was. After I had entered, I noticed that the talk had died down. I felt I was interrupting them and went to the balcony with a chair to look at what was happening in the world outside. My addictive way of spending free time was looking at what people did and learning things, some of which I compiled for special edition reports. My stepmother thought I should have taken art as my career and it was the only thing I ever heard her say as a suggestion.

Thika Road was overflowing with traffic, which was not anything unusual at that hour. We were used to it to a point where one could have made a correct guess as to what was happening at a point at a specific time. Children gathered on balconies of tall buildings to stare at the traffic mess, enjoying every bit of it as they shouted with excitement whenever a vehicle smashed another from behind. As usual a traffic policeman would be seen making space for some motorists for a fifty or twenty shillings note. The relationship between Thika Road users and policemen was symbiotic with the exchange of bribes for services. Both pedestrians and motorists were used to it so much that they did not see it as something illegal. Towards the end of the month when they were broke Thika Road policemen became sniffer dogs. They would know which vehicle carried something illegal by simply looking at it. On top of that, every vehicle they stopped had to have a mistake. The owner would part with a negotiable few hundred shillings to go on his way. In fact, by the end of the month they made money many times their salary.

Traffic started moving slowly in one of the major jams which stretched up to where the road disappeared beyond the buildings. From an aerial view it looked like a multi-coloured giant caterpillar making gradual moves by forward and sideways twitch of muscles. More than once a screech of brakes in between the lanes or sounds of breaking glass falling on the tarmac was heard. Those involved found a way of settling it without involving judicial systems. That was because there was a likelihood that the vehicles had expired insurance and fake registration numbers or, most likely, were trafficking drugs and narcotics at that hour when it was a practical impossibility to search each vehicle without creating a jam that would not clear until the following week. Even the dumbest person understood that it was cheaper to repair a broken indicator than to answer a case in court. Then as the evening ushered in darkness, floodlights lit themselves one by one along strategic places. The long line of vehicles changed to a master dragon of lights in the darkness filled with hooting alerts and angry shouting. Curls of white and black smoke moved up, slowly contaminating the air to choke the same people who started it.

The happenings of the road were covered by darkness hidden away from human witness for the sake of life itself. School girls hovered from one restaurant to the other with strangers who promised them money and fun miles away from home and guardians who thought they were in libraries and study rooms at that hour. Vegetable and fruit stalls were active at that hour as if people were caught by surprise that they needed to eat supper. They lined without a line and exchanged money for vegetables from women who reduced kales and cabbages to strands with sharp knives as their children packed them in sizes depending on cost. Speed was crucial if they wanted to maintain their business. At least they understood and that was why they were alive. The high cost of living did not allow them to work any less. Their customers kept on flowing in for fruits, not because they intended to keep healthy, but because they were cheap. The surplus supply from organic farmers, who were running at a loss, landed in the stomachs of people who never dropped a sweat for the growing seasons.

The warm air was diluted by cold currents from the north and soon the cold air was in charge. I needed to add something on top of my shirt but did not want to go to the room yet. The events out there were interesting minute after minute. Russel's mother said when we were little kids that I was selfish when it came to spending time. More wind blew, sweeping dead leaves off the fig tree outside along the ground. They made a sound like that of a rattle snake as dust particles lifted from the ground mixed with them. The clothes on the lines swayed, letting loose some of the pegs which dropped on the veranda below as the night insects started their senseless competitions of circling security bulbs. I did not understand where they obtained energy within their tiny bodies for going round and round thousands of times. It was endless, like the students below who were always walking to the rooms and libraries with books or conspiring in darkness and roaming to the capital where they stayed until they were broke.

The girl next door opened the door. She peeped along the corridor and then walked out adjusting her overcoat. She greeted me and took out a packet of cigarettes. She lit herself one and shook the packet. When I did not say anything she asked instead.

"Would you like a cigarette?"

"I don't smoke," I said with firmness.

She filled her cheeks with air and then released it airing the tip of her folded tongue.

"I did not ask you whether you smoked," she said with a stern voice.

"You should have just said no."

She was in high heels at such a late hour. Even when she was smoking her teeth were as white as a bleached paper and her beauty would have suggested harmlessness until the weight of her voice gave her away. She pocketed her left hand and let out more smoke which reluctantly sailed in the air with white curls.

"They call me Irene," she said.

"Who are they?"I asked.

"The mutual beneficiaries."

"Who are those?"

"Businessmen and merry-go-round bastards," she said sniveling.

"And what should I call you?" I asked.

"It depends."

"On what?"

She looked at me, concluded I was stupid then cleared her throat and turned to face Thika Road.

"There was a deaf person who insisted on listening to music, and he said he did not like hearing people's voices….it's complicated to think about."

The blowing wind opened the door to Irene's room. There was a drunken man on a chair not aware of himself or the changing weather. The ash tray on the table was full of cigarette butts. There were also several expensive brands of liquor on the shelf. It looked like a laboratory chemical store. Irene went and closed it then came back without caring what I thought about her. The loud music from the rooms made windows vibrate; making anyone who was walking along the balcony shout to be heard. Girls called each other at the top of their voices in the next female block, sharing affairs gossip and giggling as they dragged slippers on the floors on their way to the toilets with tissues in their hands. The echo sent their high-pitched laughs penetrating ears like amplified lunch bells. Irene struggled to sneeze without success. She put the back of her gloved hand on her nostrils to soothe them.

The catering and accommodations staff allocated rooms to the best of their expertise, but soon the arrangements were altered. As students turned into love birds and saw no need of staying alone. The girls crossed over to the male hostels to experiment with being young families. They would look so practical that they believed they were like married couples. The boys would sit on chairs reading magazines and newspapers while the girls did the cooking and served them food which they shared. They would then wash their clothes and iron them after which they neatly folded and put them in the wardrobes. They would massage them, and when they got bored with the rooms they walked to the nature zones with drinks and snacks to spend time waiting for darkness. In the mornings the girls would wake up earlier and ask for money to buy breakfast items and prepare 'breakfast for two' to start the day. It was tempting to try but people like me with experiences here and there knew that some things were not as sweet as they looked. I had seen it countless times at the school of journalism but had never come across a girl who owned a room in male hostels like Irene did.

Then as I looked at her in silence bats flew low and cleared the insects which circled the bulbs. It took seconds before they appeared again from a hidden supply. There was a loud explosion from the direction of the students centre. A group of boys had staged a fight so that they would gain access to free food and drinks. Beer bottles and flying objects missing targets were hitting against the walls. Windows flew open and those who felt they had missed the occasion put on whatever their hands could grab and rushed out to join the rest of the hooligans. The security vehicle arrived on time and thwarted the mess, leaving disappointed vandals watching from a distance. It was easy to lose track of days in college because such lifestyles made a stranger think people were on holiday. It was difficult to tell it was a weekday by simply looking at the activities, which was the reason why those who cared had calendars stuck on their walls and reminders switched on all the time.

"It's this way it is here each and every day," Irene said, looking far away beyond the horizon where the capital's lighting illuminated the sky.

She extinguished the cigarette by pressing it between the thumb and forefinger then turned away from the cantilevers.

"You have a feeling that what is happening out there is madness, huh?"

"Yes," I said.

"They know what they are doing. Only they're doing it wrongly," she said.

"What you are seeing is only a clue of what actually happens," she went on to explain.

"There is no such a thing as time and season for everything here. What surprises me is why it is your business," she said, following my eyes that were on a boy holding the hands of two girls.

She was familiar with what was happening out there and observant on what I thought in a way I did not understand. She did not turn to look at the commotion whenever it happened down there, like someone who had seen it for several years until it made no sense. Students stood and moved in pairs to any corner as long as there was something interesting happening. When there was no action at all, they became action themselves by driving themselves into fantasies under the cover of darkness in various rooms. Those under the scare of examinations moved to the libraries and grasped a few points. By so doing, they armed themselves with something they could write on the mid semester examinations, before they moved out to join the rest of the merry makers. They felt they had missed the fun, which they claimed if they did not have that time then they would never have it any other time. One by one they left the libraries driven by temptations of cell phone messages that told them that they had missed something and needed to be somewhere else. The librarians were left yawning with boredom and fatigue while staring at books on the tables and shelves and looking at their watches every five minutes, impatient for closing time.

The moon and the stars appeared high in the sky giving soft light down to the people who did not need it. It was as pointless as trying to burn down a house using hot water. All nights were similar and it was the only phenomenon which was not a component of weather standing solidly free of man and his pointless activities. Stars moved closer in sizes like children listening to war stories of their grandfather, the moon, around the fire in an African night. Those who loved each other took their time in the half-light, calling it a romantic time because it was the way other everybody else did it. They called the people they loved 'honey,' 'medication' or anything nice they thought of. The students were notorious with the trend and stopped at nothing to do it in such a place where their hands were not tied to constant voice reminders of those who were supposed to take care of them. They exercised what they saw on television soap operas in dark corridors and shadows of structures smearing them with emotions which made it almost real. Surprisingly, sooner or later they found out that there was no such a thing as living happily ever after.

When I went back inside, I found Meyer alone washing his hands in the sink bare chested. The chocolate tin was on the floor and his bed looked disturbed. The curtain was pulled down and one chair was facing the door. He wiped his hands on the back of his baggy jean shorts and went to dry them with the towel hanging from the nail on the wall. He then went to spend some time looking in the mirror, admiring his teeth and twisting his mouth to different directions to have a keen look at his young beard. When he was not satisfied with his looks he fetched a comb and started brushing his hair gently. He was always conscious about his looks, and there was never a single day I saw him rush out with the carelessness of men who were in the habit of getting out of bed fifteen minutes before a lesson in college. He was a kind of man who would have sent any girl interested in him cautious because his things were always neat. As hard as he tried to care for his looks it occurred to me with a simple observation that he was the laziest person I knew when it came to washing utensils. He would avoid cooking as long as the dirty utensils were in the sink.

The room did not lie about Meyer. It made me feel like a stranger whenever I was in it. There were huge photos of scantily dressed girls on the opposite walls. An Adolf Hitler caricature holding to a riffle covered half the wall facing the door where a door curtain opened to my room. There were several model magazines on the table where one exercise book written in Japanese, *Hiragana* and *kanji*, was open beside another which was closed with a pen in between. With the curiosity of a journalist, I went through some of the magazines of course to see if there would be something which interested me. There was a female blue school uniform neatly folded in his open suit case. There was also something which confused me about first impressions; which proved to be false years later. The dazzling trophy presented to him as the most disciplined boy back in his high school.

Chapter Two

The frogs of Thika Road and beyond were on riot with a well-coordinated croaking as if they were drunk from the early morning drizzle. They would have croaked a corpse into life. A sudden disruption sent them quiet but once the king bullfrog gave the signal, they resumed like a thousand snoring men. One would have feared for another frog miracle. It was not the passing of a vehicle which scared them but noise from a tyre burst or an explosion from a smelting industry. Cats of Thika Road were sleeping on their predation job and they would have illustrated the true meaning of domesticated animals. They drank the milk of their masters and waited for pet food in the evening, playing with the frogs only when they felt like exercising. The nature pond beyond the block had also teamed up with the other amphibians without manners to disturb the human populated environment with no second thought that they were in a foreign language institution which called for hospitality for the sake of good international relations.

The conservationists and environmentalists said they wanted the frogs left alone for future generations. They claimed natural mechanisms were enough to take care of the tremendous populations. I did not know what the meaning of that was because there was nothing natural along Thika Road. Not even the way life itself was supported. As anybody living along Thika Road would have said, the true meaning of survival was to be present in risk but avoid getting involved. A bullfrog would inflate its cheeks in the middle of the road with speeding vehicles while crossing and still make it to the other side. Taking advantage of the people's laxity they penetrated little spaces under doors and slept luxuriantly under anything warm they found in houses. They did not mind then finding enough manners to maintain silence until they were discovered. A woman living nearby discovered a cooked frog in the serving bowl at the end of a meal; it had jumped into meat soup while it was cooking on the stove thinking it was just water.

My roommate, Meyer, swept with a broom a little frog which resisted to stay outside and then came back to his seat where he had been roasting meat. He was a carnivore when it came to meat regardless of time, and I feared he would develop gout if he was not careful. The warmth of the charcoal burner maintained life and kept mosquitoes away on such a cold morning when everyone was turning on his bed with regrets of where they left the previous day's unfinished work. I personally did not touch meat except in limited social situations. This was after my grandfather joked when I was a just a little kid that the stomach of a human being is not a grave for burying dead things. It filled my mind with weird images, which changed my attitude towards meat even when I became an adult. I was sitting on my bed reading an outdated news roundup about a man who was beaten to death by his wife with a shoe for wearing her pants. Even when some things sounded funny their real existence was evident. The media was good because it brought them to the light for everyone to know.

"There is this song which says that heaven and hell are similar things turned inside out. You know it?" Meyer asked.

"Yes," I said.

He stared at the wall. I anticipated a question about the song which did not come.

"What about it?" I asked closing the newspaper.

"The singer must be a critical thinker," he said with his eyes on the wall.

"What makes you think like that?"

"Because he is. Some things do not have simplified explanations."

"Maybe they do. I disagree," I said.

"You do not have to," he said licking his lips.

"You know, Brooks, the world will not stop if you cease to exist. See? You will be fighting nature and as anybody who understands it will tell you it will be the same as fighting a losing battle."

He looked at me with his face prepared to accept that I intended to disagree with whatever he wanted to say. He was right. I knew that some people brought forward correct explanations to justify their wrong theories.

"It depends on what you want to believe," he said.

"There was this rich American preacher who shouted that his life and property was under spiritual protection, but when he became bankrupt he changed to some tune like earthy wealth does not guarantee heavenly kingdom. A year later he died from careless driving and if interrogated in death he would have said something about the uselessness of life."

"You never cease to amaze me," I said and shrugged.

He scratched his head and then caressed his nose, half closing his eyes from the smoke.

"Maybe I can."

He put the meat into a plate and then moved the charcoal burner to the far corner.

"You have been looking at me and saying he has too many girls, huh?"

"Yes," I said.

"It has all along been in human history. The kings and those other men who made headlines. You think owning a lot of women was a victory waiting for stupid men like me?"

He laughed mockingly wiping his eyes with the back of his hand.

"The problem is not what I do. The problem is you and those others suffering from insanity of understanding. Making life something better to talk about does not mean you close your eyes to the realities about it, no matter how ugly they look."

"What are those realities?"

"It would be pointless to make you understand. There were two dogs which argued about what happened to the food they ate. One dog ate its own shit claiming they were remnants of undigested food. When famine came, the other one followed suit. You now understand between the two which one was laughing then."

"They were just dogs," I said.

He looked at me for a time then blinked one of his eyes several times.

"Can I ask you a question?"

"Yes," I said.

"Every man thinks about a woman at some point, right?"

"Yes," I replied.

"Good," he said licking his lips.

"You are running away from yourself, Portuguese man. Your mind is filled with laughable laws explaining how you can separate yourself from your shadow. You think like me but you pretend to be different in your actions. Same theory, different practicals, see?"

"What do you mean 'I think like you'?"

I asked him a little annoyed.

"Because both of us are men, Brooks."

He was a person who insisted all people thought similar towards wickedness. Strange still he believed it with ready explanations formulated in his mind, which were attached with proof and simplification. His intoxicated mind was the centre of processing whatever his actions revealed. No one would have believed it unless they saw it with their own eyes. If a documentary about him were made and aired to an audience, the audience would have forgotten that they were watching a documentary and assumed that they were watching a sexual affair movie. There was another side of the story. One from those girls who always flocked around him regardless of having sufficient information about the kind of a person they were dealing with.

Like the girl, Eve, they lied to themselves with him in turns and hit their chests about the kind of heroes they were, talking about how handsome he looked on their photos.

"Each person lies to himself or herself when they have second thoughts," he said.

"The only thing that discovers the lie is reality which hacks them down using it. Winning on one side is losing on the other."

His words flowed from quick memory which he retrieved when need arose. He cut a piece of meat and threw it into his mouth then looked at me while chewing.

"Anything which eats a dead thing dies to be eaten. It might run or even hide but that does not go on for too long. So you can see it is easier to sit and say what will become is what shall become and that is the way it is, Mr. Portugal."

There was no single person in the rain when I looked outside the window. Only dogs crossing from one building to the other or fighting for food in the grass and flower beds. The carnivores emerged in numbers bigger and fatter during the rains from a secret place. Impatient workers stood outside offices and other structures of shelter looking at their watches, which seemed to tick faster, ready for the slightest indication when the rain would stop. The classes had few students who were held inside by the rain for the early morning lessons and regretted their decisions. They crossed to nearby resource centres to read magazines and journals. As usual, most students kept to their rooms with their partners for warmth in such weather. This fuelled reproduction and copulation experiments whose results were little accepted even by the owners of their own engineering.

At the first stop of the rain, people poured into the streets. They did not wait for the icy droplets to clear. Time was money and that was what they were losing. Thika Road traffic was going at a snail's pace. Impatient drivers taking children to school looked at their watches and leaned behind steering wheels, fearing for their jobs. They cursed loudly and hooted carelessly at those in front who allowed overtaking cars too manouvre in the traffic standoff. Those early risers transporting construction materials with black smoked old trucks were on the road too. The casual workers hooded themselves with dirty and torn old overcoats claiming to maintain their temperatures by sharing cigarette puffs. They put them off whenever they felt enough tobacco had reached their lungs because they were not yet sure of the day. Hungry youths and school drop outs loitering around were on high alert for casual labour demands to provide them with daily bread. Cheap tea rooms for such people hurried up charcoal burners with old bucket leads in the open to avoid breakfast frustrations during the business hours.

Even as a crushed dog lay on the road from the previous night, flattened and chirred by moving rubber, nobody had the time to look at what happened because as someone would learn soon it was because they were part of it. Not ready to risk being crushed, hungry crows walked away and eagles flew around and perched on structures waiting for traffic to clear so that they could have their fill and spend the day mating in the trees and shitting on people's heads. I remember a professor who was decorated with white droppings in the open when I was in journalism school, just as he was shouting at someone to stop interrupting his lecture. Instead of wiping his face sideways, he pushed it towards the nose and moustache. With a disgusted creased face, he looked like an old colobus monkey. Those birds were multiplying at abnormal rates in specific areas. When there were no animal bodies on the road to scavenge on, they flew around butcheries or terrorised women selling foodstuffs, especially fish, at the side of the road. -Adaptive as they became it was almost an impossibility to kill a bird along Thika Road. They read intentions and flew away long before one picked a stone.

It started drizzling again first in tiny drops scattering sand and breaking away compact mud. The water flew on the tarmac, splashing with tiny drops which accumulated enough to form a surface runoff that swept the crushed dog fragments and raw soup down to a well where women and children were busy taking water sold to the cafes for making tea, which people paid to enjoy especially in such a cold morning. The people made themselves understand that the tea they were taking was not dog because their pockets did not permit thinking otherwise. The collective responsibility of poverty brought them together and drinking the tea without asking questions was the only means of maintaining oneself when the corners of the month moulded their tummies. That was why they never stayed away. When no one got ill or died from the tea, more customers flocked the tea rooms. They brought more money which made the owners keep smiling all the way to the bank.

Away from the bigger community, outside college, there was the student community who felt that they were miles away from the people out there, like the moon from the surface of the earth. They felt they did not share anything except being humans, maybe, and humans had their differences. They did not talk to them along passenger picking points and saw them as people who were misled both by themselves and situations. Then as they peeped through windows, having been tired from the late morning of the day which had refused to open its eyelids. They felt secure from the previous night, thinking that unlearned people were from out there, who were employed as watchmen, were servants who needed to make sure they had a good night and would have a nice day. Some students from poor families knew what learning through hardship meant, but to many others who were able to bask in the wealth of their guardians, they thought the stories they heard about starving communities and the things they read and saw in the media about that part of the world, which existed by the grace of God, was like an edited documentary or a movie on extreme poverty. The concern about how life existed was not knowing or seeing but learning from what different situations meant. As it happened more than often, that is what the students did not do.

The noisy girl of the next block was busy washing her clothes outside her closed front door on the balcony in the stormy morning, singing an irritating local tune with a stinging sound. Her voice penetrated the adjacent blocks and beyond, loud and clear above the drizzle. She would have been helpful for anyone who wanted to carry out experiments about sound because her voice easily penetrated concrete walls making the stomachs of those who were easily annoyed secrete acid. I used to wonder whether somewhere along her life someone had ever told her that she needed to mind others, even when she was blessed with lungs of such great elasticity. There was someone, probably her roommate, who was telling her something probably unfunny, but all I could hear was her laughing like ringing lunch bells. According to my roommate, Meyer, she could keep children awake the whole night when she became a mother. There was a rumour across the block that she did not struggle to achieve the top grades in class, but I did not know how that distinguished value helped the rest of us. When she broke into another tune, Meyer closed the window.

He went back to his chair and tried to kill a spider crossing the floor using his foot. The spider made it with dashing speed and climbed the wall then paused some distance from the floor as if to rest and think. Meyer picked a slipper from under the bed and pinned it on the wall with a well-timed slap. It stuck dry to the wall as if it had existed ages ago with its brown juices making an ugly mark on the lower side. He cut a piece of tissue paper and cleaned the wall then threw it in the rubbish bucket. He took a magnifying lens from the shelf and observed the spot like a forensic scientist.

"There is no life after death," he said.

He frowned then creased his face before he closed his eyes and took a deep breath.

"You know, I have never understood appearance and reality, man," he said licking his lips.

"Really?" I asked, hoping he would keep quiet.

"I think those philosophers were madmen of their own cause," he continued.

"My elder sister and her fiancée brought shame to themselves and our family yet stood their ground by breaking up in a shopping mall four days before their wedding. Sounds crazy, doesn't it? You know what other people thought? They thought that they did not have enough reasons for doing so but according to me they did. When I later thought about it, I realised that it was for a stupid reason."

"What did they do?" I asked.

"They agreed to test their compatibility by closing their eyes and picking at random from a refrigerator containing water and juice. When he picked water and she picked juice, they interpreted that as them having nothing in common, so they parted ways."

"Why did you disagree with their choice?" I asked.

"To make a dovetail joint you need a dovetailed wood and its socket. I want you to think of what it would be like if everyone were to think similarly and have the same likes and dislikes. Would there ever be a need to come together?"

He caressed his hairy right leg then straightened his trouser.

"I'm not saying people should do things in imitation for the reason that there should be someone pulling in the opposite direction but it happens anyway. When there is richness, the other side should reflect poverty and when there is life, there should be death and so on."

"It's not always with every situation. However few, some cases have gotten intermediates," I said.

"That is the point," he said as if he was waiting for it.

"Things are set in such a way that if a person gets this he misses the other. With richness there are classes, and with poverty there are levels. The struggle for betterment is the basis of change. In other words, a victor can never exist without a victim."

The blowing wind threatened to break tree canopies outside, but their efforts were compressed to plucking few leaves and pushing them through the air and on the ground, then depositing them in ridges and balconies as well as pavements and corridors. It then showed its anger for the unyielding effort by banging windows and blowing over papers on tables in the rooms. The season of strong winds was beckoning because at the end of every phase it left trees bending to its direction. Somewhere in the old trees a branch would break giving rise to many others a few days after. That was the same way Meyer sprouted theories and stories in his mind and told them to me, not because he wanted me to see how deep he would think, but to show that he was serious about what he said. Every day he came up with something new and he knew how to make someone disinterested listen to what he was saying. The winds blowing to the east might have gone with what he took out of his mouth but the rains and dust settled in his mind with the same theories and other endless brand new developments awaiting implementation.

Anyone who was living along Thika Road would have testified that rainfall was never an advantage, apart from cooling down dust and watering scarce clay soils, which were not anywhere near supporting agricultural activities. Those who benefitted were capitalists who took advantage of its occurrence for personal gains. As I stood looking at the people nursing frustrations under shelters, commuter buses hiked prices knowing the people would pay anyway. Sharpness called for proper estimations between time and weather along the road if one needed to pay a lower fare. Workers at construction sites were already budgeting unyielding mathematics in their minds having known they were going to receive half pay at the end of the day. As it was always, their frustrations soon turned to creativity which seized opportunities. On the first drop, rain coats and umbrellas appeared along passenger picking points and shelters as if the hawkers knew it would rain. Demand shot high because of women's needs, which led to doubling of prices and inevitably making people frown and crease their faces. Consumers would close their eyes as they purchased necessary items under one of these situations. They would buy anyway in one of the situations they described as paying while closing the eyes.

At the first stop of the rainfall, I grabbed my bag and walked into the humid morning. There was some sense of purpose then after the previous night's partying and excitement. The stormy weather did not prevent girls from wearing tiny skirts and bare backs. The cemented pavements spared them the agony of their high-heeled shoes sinking in the saturated soils. Everyone seemed to realise then that apart from what went on in darkness and hidden places, books had given them the gate pass to such a place which called for respect whenever anyone learning in it stood to speak to any audience. As most attention shifted to the girls whenever they passed, even the boys were in their best that morning. There were some who took the trouble of wearing suits for just a single lesson a day. They looked nice in them but wasted a lot of time preparing them. They could be seen practicing what they saw in movies and fashion shows by faking springy walks with the day's newspapers; whose contents they had no idea.

Mrs. Fabiano was already in class waiting for students to arrive. She was among the women I knew who drove heavy vehicles. The simplest way to know if she was in class was to look for her Range Rover in the parking lot. When I entered she raised her eyebrows in greetings. She had a sharp memory and did not need to search for long to remember me.

"Good morning Mrs. Fabiano," I greeted her.

"Good morning, Ishimwe," she answered.

"Did you go through that hand-out?"

"Yes," I said, sitting down.

"How do you say good morning in Portuguese?"

"*Bom dia senhora Fabiano?*"

"Next time I expect you to use that."

Learning a language from the first step was like that of a baby learning to speak. I understood that because I was a parent. I put into memory everything I observed Russel do and that would guide me on how I was supposed to handle him when teaching him about ethics. Nurturing a young person in an environment that pulled in the opposite direction was difficult, like preventing a climbing plant from using its tendrils. When I was honest with myself, I felt that I did not possess any concrete surety that the ways I was teaching him would stick. Being just a young adult, I did what I hated doing by attaching what I taught him with a question of time. I knew that as long as he was with me he would do whatever I told him, be anything I wanted, but soon he would grow to be a teenager and go to social adventures out there. New things and new places brought excitation like that of a zero grazed calf which broke free. I wanted Russel to develop independent thinking as he grew up because I had seen what thinking for someone did to the adult life. It was like releasing a fingerling without experience into a pond of fish eating-snakes.

One thing I had learnt having stayed with students for a long time was that most of them did not know there was very little difference between dreams and their lives in future tense. I knew that I read too many books of philosophy and psychology as well as those inspirational ones whose authors my father referred to as insane. He had a special hatred for white skin coloured people, except the engineering products they made. He used to tell me that there were enough authors in the country whenever he found me reading anything from Western countries. One day I demanded to know why he was always against white skinned people. That's when I discovered that he was a racist. To him, it did not matter where anyone came from as long as their skin was not white. An Irish volunteer teacher beat him up and branded him 'the drum' in elementary school after he failed to speak a simple sentence, no matter how long he repeated it. What the teacher meant was that a drum was a dead thing and the only thing which symbolised its existence was the sound it made when beating it.

Mrs. Fabiano split us into pairs that morning, and we practiced conversations with as many basic phrases as possible. I was paired with the soft spoken girl, Tracy, whose tragic end taught me that there always existed an element of bad luck which was the only explanation as to why some things happened. She was the only girl I knew in all my years at college who understood the meaning of life the same way I did, and she was the only person who struck me with a sense of purpose that is difficult to explain even years after her death. After the lesson that morning, we went for tea down at the cafeteria, battling the weather which had stood to its ground the whole morning. I expected that she would soon learn that I was never excited by anything in particular and quit first, but she was a kind of person who left people and their characters alone. One of the things which I was never born with was the natural inclination to smile, even when amused, which was scary to many people, girls in particular, who soon learnt to respect my required distance. My grandfather used to say I took after his younger bachelor brother who had since died by a bonfire in a house fire.

"He had eyes that popped out of their sockets like those of a goat," he said.

"Was that the reason why he never married?" I asked him.

"Not really. It was one of the reasons though. Women used to say he was scary and one could never tell if he was in the mood of strangling someone."

I laughed.

"He was a hardworking person though, and there was never a single day his farm was infested with weeds."

He looked into the air as if looking for the right words for my age before he continued.

"Even though he never married, I do not think it was a good thing to stay in an empty house like that."

He said, and then pushed the logs deeper into the fire.

"After he died his farm quickly became infested with weeds. Look at who now tills his farm," he said grinding his teeth.

"Strangers and the wives of his brothers."

He talked with regret and sadness.

"It is not a good thing to stay unmarried," he added.

"Is it a good thing to marry?" I asked him.

He looked at me and I saw sympathy register on his face. He knew that I was referring to the family I grew up in after my mother died; we lived like roommates. Everyone woke up to do things which suited him best and the only time we gathered was when we were solving conflicts. He patted my shoulder softly and looked me in the eyes.

"Yes, my boy," he said.

"Marriage is a good thing and when you will come of age you will understand that."

He looked at the earth wall and shook his head several times. He then mumbled something incomprehensible whose weight I could only see with the movement in his old throat. He started singing a song of the past which talked about grandmother's millet, and only then did he remember his old traditional drum made from wood and leopard skin and went to fetch it. He played and tried to cheer me up by telling me to dance to the rhythm but when I refused he rose up slowly like an aged rooster supporting his tired back and then demonstrated by shaking his shoulders and waving his hands until I burst out laughing and joined him.

Tracy had a special love for children, especially the orphans and those in the streets. She came to know about Russel one day when I was making a call home to find out how he was doing, and from that moment on she asked me how he was doing whenever we met. Her consistency of looking at things dove eyed, especially humanity, could have only been compared to that of Faith, the black-fated girl who stepped into the world like a princess but died like a leper and was buried like a dog. Unlike those two girls, I had made too many changes along my life that if asked I would not be able to describe what my original view about life was then. The fast changing world was changing everyone and everything for better or for worse. According to Tracy, if there would have been an underground interview, very few people would have said that they had lived their lives to the fullest before they died. She quoted several examples of people who suffered on their way to making wealth and fame but died before they could even experience it. So she decided to approach life differently by dedicating hers to other people.

Our lives were hanging in the delicate times of Africa, the continent which suffers from hunger, poverty and disease. The fear of the 'insect', which was a street name for a pandemic that arrived ages ago by ships and planes to show the fury of nature, was all over. The dread was given the name because of the way it reduced people to frames like insects did to wood. Any miscalculated step sent someone coming down in tumbles. It was a natural means of reducing the ever increasing population, and those studying population trends and economists were not surprised because they understood the reasons behind those natural means of regulating a population. According to what they said, the high population was bad for the economy but to the rest of us who tended to cling to life, it was either assisting the economy grow or fall without prior knowledge of what had happened. The same way everyone remembers their first love experience which stores itself in an inerasable part of the brain, whenever I thought about the insect, Russel's mother appeared in my mind as if I was just a child the previous day and the years had been stagnant.

Faith was a girl who became both a sister and a mother to me having lost my most fundamental psychologist: my mother. I can say above everything she was a friend. Although we were of an almost similar age, because I was born just a month before she was born, she always took on the responsibility and reasoning of a much older person, unlike me. At times I can admit to my embarrassment of laxity. She and her aunt Rebecca had come to settle at our semi-permanent apartments as tenants after both her parents were killed by wild animals while carrying out research in the heart of the Maasai Mara. The wealth of her parents was seized by her numerous uncles and she was ejected from the family after they alleged that there was no biological relationship between her and the father. She lived there for years with her aunt who worked as a house keeper in the neighbouring compound .She used to come to our compound to jump rope with me or juggle with the small rounded stones we collected from the road. If there was anything to go by then, I think if she lived her life longer than she did, she would have been a reliable choice for a social worker. She used to take out the beddings I wetted and spread them outside in the sun to dry and would remind me to take them back to the house when the rain was about to fall or she would even do it for me. Sometimes she hid biscuits in her pockets and gave them to me when we went out to play.

Having lost my mother when I was very young and growing up knowing Faith during my childhood, the days grew long when they moved from our apartments. I grew up at a time when there were no other kids close to my age in the neighbourhood to spend time with. My younger sister was crawling at the time and our domestic worker was a middle-aged man who was half deaf, and unless one shouted he would not have heard. He spent time with our numerous cows in the fields or sometimes went weeding crops near the river. My father was never at home during the daytime, but I must admit that I was glad because he had a tendency of pointing out mistakes every time he was around. He would never miss something undone and would spend a couple of minutes talking about how dissatisfied he was. As far as I could remember, his happiness disappeared when mother died and

I could count the number of times I saw him light up his face with a smile. He was always at war with my step-mother, who accused him of incompetence in bringing up the family. He never said a word whenever she was talking but I could tell he was not okay because whenever that happened he put on his hat and walked out with a machete to inspect our farm.

Years came and went. I grew into a teenager who was willing to take life the way it came. One night when I was about to go to bed someone knocked on the door. I usually did not respond to such knocks because I knew it was our houseboy Tom who wanted me to help him restrain one of the cows that had uprooted a tether and strayed to the bean farms. He had a never ending habit of erecting weak tethers. He usually shouted something angry seconds after and went away but when nobody spoke I went to open the door. I was surprised when I saw Faith standing there. The smile I had registered melted away. The security light lit her fleshless frame. She was reduced to a skeletal structure covered by skin, different from the heavy bodied girl I knew years before. With a baby in her hands, she shook like a pneumonia stricken lamb. When I welcomed her in she took two steps and almost tripped. I took the baby with the composure of the young man I was becoming. Soon that composure melted away sensing everything was not okay, even when I did not know what was wrong.

Sitting there looking at Faith, I could not find a better scene to describe human suffering. I saw that she still had the motherly understanding she commanded in childhood. She told me not to worry and even lit her dilapidated face with a smile. She had the courage and determination I found difficult to compare yet it failed to convince me that things were to be the same again. Her sleeping baby was in complete contrast, fat and brown playing with her fingers inside a warm jacket and moving his lips like a new-born kitten fumbling for teats under its mother's fur. We sat without speaking for a time, not because there was nothing to say, but because there were hundreds of questions revolving in my mind without answers. She decided to break the silence because she had come to me and looked prepared for it. When she told me what happened to her over the years her voice was shaky and her eyes teary from disease and regret.

Faith married a man whom she hoped would free her from poverty and the emptiness she felt. The man claimed to work in one of the firms in Nairobi but she did not know whether that was true when they met in the outskirts of the city. At that time it did not matter what one was doing in Nairobi. The mention of the city brought with it pride and prestige which would have easily tempted anyone of Faith's status. Like unfolding the events of ugly scenes, she later discovered she was just a love-girl who was used like a plaything for fulfilling the man's pleasures. She was later abandoned in a lonely house when she told him that she was pregnant, thinking it was good news for a newly married couple. Whenever things failed to work for women in their marriages as they tried to settle, the only place they thought about was home. Those who were there might have disagreed with their marriage choices and decisions made in the past but surely they would receive them. For a young girl who did not have anything called home, she decided to go back to her aunt and hoped she would forgive her and understand what had happened. When she discovered the pregnancy she evicted her, and she spent days wandering from house to house seeing whether there was something she could do for a living.

"I would have helped you Faith," I told her.

She stared at the wall.

"You should have told me."

One thing I discovered, although I understood that the best way to become a man with time was growing up like one, was that there were situations which made men women. A man can boast about the large amount of pepper he can swallow but he cannot accommodate the smallest amount in his eyes. I let my tears flow free when she mentioned that above all, the man had infected her with the insect. There were no more games like those from our childhood. There would be no jumping rope or image guessing in the pages of the Bible story books. The last time I felt like that was when my mother died and it took me years to understand what her dying meant. She did not shed a tear but spoke with a composed voice the way she always did. Her time was up and she understood that. She had come to request me take care of her baby. She did not listen no matter how much I persuaded her to stay. She seemed to have made up her mind and said she was going to *Clemência de Deus,* a mission hospital which was across the river.

My most immediate concern was to find out the status of the little angel. I was overjoyed when I took him for testing and he tested HIV negative. He was the only hope of Faith and her family who needed to live if a tale about their family would have been told in the future. I did not even know whether that future existed but it was always up to me to do my best. Such were the untold stories of young lives which took rugged trends, before tragedies struck and extinguished lights of bright futures. Someone needed to care but it was unknown whether that would have been a possibility in the near future. Children were angels, and that was what my mother made me understand by the sweet things she always did for us when she was alive. I would have done anything for Faith in life or in death. I did have an opportunity to see her in her hospital bed for the last time.

When she died two weeks later, I attended the funeral at her deserted mother's home. There was nothing one would relate to because the grandparents were long dead. Faith's burial did not have anything one would have called the 'last respects.' There were a limited number of volunteers who wanted to dig her grave and so I joined them. Women and girls stood arms akimbo at a distance, gossiping and making up stories about what led to her death. They avoided going near the body because of infection theories which originated among themselves. It would soon spread among the groups like fire on petrol and then they would tell it to their mates as if they were philosophical doctors on epidemics and pandemics. There were also those men who considered themselves heroes for sleeping with 'clean' girls and went ahead to describe with obscene details to the others how they did it. They talked as long as there were ears to listen. The Portuguese father, Agostinho Alberto, who was a key figure behind the establishment of the mission hospital, read a scripture which was listened to then more than any other time. He described what came from soil as what went back to it.

Chapter Three

The role an actor perfects is not very different from reality. However, she or he must not admit it to the audience for the sake of their career. Irene confirmed this when she decided to deliberately leak her secret life to me. I knew too well that as an experienced trickster there was likely to be a sinister motive behind her actions. I was a complete stranger to her, but she considered me a kind stranger and she was wrong. Her naivety worked in my favour. It was barely a month after a human rights activist was forced to apologize for calling women the most dangerous biological weapon against men after a mass of women's groups took to the streets to demonstrate. As a journalist I was always updated about those things, but as difficult as it was, I always tried to learn from them. I understood that one did not need to do something special to trigger activists against his life after I filed stories about casual labourers who were strangled on their way from work so that others would get the jobs which cost about seventy shillings a day.

The wisest thing a person of my caution should have done when she invited me to her room was to turn down the invitation and cut all links of communication between me and her, but I thought otherwise when I remembered I needed to compile something about the 'two faces' of students and workers in college. Separating curiosity and stubbornness from a journalist is like trying to prevent a cow from eating grass. Deep inside I knew I was not playing dumb. The secret to survival in my career, when dealing with people like those in our country, was to always know more than anybody else and make multiple interpretations and take precautions before anything happened. If I fell into trouble then it needed to be under extremely unavoidable circumstances. That was the basis of survival as a journalist in my country during those times. Many others like me had gone undercover after a member of the freelance journalist club was found dead deep in Karura Forest with his hands and genitals missing.

The story of Irene, the free smoking girl would have sounded like a morality narration meant to scare children into learning a lesson. The problem with the story would have been that she was rarely a victim and ended up a bad character who went unpunished. Anybody listening to it would have concluded in their mind that it never existed, long before the narration was over. The most spectacular thing one would have identified her with was that she was rarely in the company of other girls. Her company was that of elderly men and it did not take long before one realised they were not students. An inexperienced person would have assumed it to be the usual game girls played away from home but I surely knew there was smoke and mirrors behind her lifestyle. For the time I had stayed there I realised that she did not miss lessons whenever she was around. She almost led a normal student life but I did not see her enter the room or leave it without a man. As a matter of fact she never left anyone in her room. I remember her dragging a drunken man out of the room and then locking the door before she went to attend class. I knew very well that if someone was associated with trouble but was never in it then they probably caused it for others.

Irene's room would have been compared to that of
the daughter of a very prominent person. Her floor had
a thick, expensive carpet on which an imported shoe
rack stood at the corner. On it were about fifty pairs
of classic shoes and one of the pairs had a diamond
coat. She was not as careless as I thought because
her room was odourless, despite the fact that she was
associated with tobacco like food was to a plate. I did
not know how she managed to replace the college
bed with a luxuriant low lying one which was spread
with a beautiful duvet. A gold necklace glittered from
a hook on the wall on which her photographs hung
where she posed like a model. Her wardrobe had a
collection of expensive dresses which were known to
exist in boutiques frequented by tourists and classy
people. One would easily tell that she liked cooking
from six gas ovens, which were unnecessary for a
student. The upper shelf had several bottles of rare
wines and spirits. It looked like a pub. There was an
ash tray on the window half full of cigarette butts.
I was beginning to suspect Irene sold drugs as well,
which I found out many days later was not the case.

It was not something easy to own things like Irene or
lead an expensive life a few kilometres from the capital
city without a well-paying job. There was a time when
my grandfather blasted my uncle in a disagreement
when my uncle boasted that he owned several pieces
of land and a motorcycle after he refused to bring up a
family at an advanced age. He told him that a person
can develop for the worse and equated it to the growth
of a country under dictation. I did not think Irene's
case was different and like my grandfather, I saw her
becoming creative by thinking in the wrong direction.
I was deep in thought when Irene lit a cigarette and I
felt the first stinging effects of tobacco in my nostrils.
I rubbed them and sneezed. When she noticed it she

went and opened the windows then put the cigarette out by knocking the lit end on the side of the ash tray until the glow died. She went and made tea and fried eggs then opened the cupboard and came with a packet of biscuits. She easily opened it with her long nails and poured them on the tray. Like a gangster can be a good mother, Irene was a good cook although one would have thought that she had no time for thinking about making nice food.

She took a fat photo album from the wardrobe and handed it over to me. The first thing I noted was that the album was arranged from the old black and white photos to the recent ones. She would have worked in a record keeping section without letting employers down. The first page had a photo of a man wearing an old school shirt with big collars and a bell bottomed trouser. He had handsome long hair combed to the back, and although he stood in big sandals which looked like those worn by the disciples in the Bible stories, he still looked nice. I pulled out the photo and looked at it from behind. It was labelled with the date it was taken in black pen and the words *father of someone* written below the date. I flipped the pages taking time with every photo, especially those of the past when she was still young. In contrast to what I thought, I found out that Irene grew up like any other emaciated African child, playing in the mud with those cheap second-hand dresses which the West loved so much to dump in our continent. She was not the voluptuous lady who sat in front of me then.

Perhaps one thing that was hard to believe then was that Irene had bushy eyebrows when she was young. Every time I saw bushy eyebrows I remembered my aunt who used to call me a cat whenever she was teasing me because I had bushy, black eyebrows. My baby sister Eunice used to laugh all day whenever I said that those women who shaved theirs leaving thin lines above their eyes looked like grasshoppers. The free smoking girl before me then looked like one giant grasshopper, with the lines above her eyes, which were extended with an eye pencil. She was drastically different from the little girl in the photos. There were several photos taken with friends in high school and various trips to the parks in the wild. Even when one would have thought Irene never achieved anything on merit, one of the photos in the album caught my attention. It was when she was being awarded a trophy for being the best Girl Guide in the district. My suspicions tallied with the trophy I had seen when she opened the wardrobe. It made me remember the words on Meyer's trophy which were hard to believe from what I knew about him. After I was done with the photos I realised that she did not have even one photo of her mother.

After I was done with the album she went and brought ten diary books and put them on the table. Even the old ones still had their covers on. She began writing diaries when she was seven and the language she used at the time was cloquent. It occurred to me that I had never thought of writing a diary. Like any other person who grew up like me, most of the things I would have put down on paper would have been disheartening. However, that did not mean I stopped thinking about them. I just let important memories stick in my head; both good, like the day I received an award for being the best student in the district, and sad, like the day my mother died. Many others like me never celebrated birthdays because competition between poverty and basic needs made them lose meaning. I remember knowing the exact day when I was born at the time I was about to request for an identity card. My father was a bad record keeper and every time I asked him the day I was born he lowered his head thinking but could not remember. I did not know why he did not go to the hospital to confirm with the records. I reminded him a couple of times but when he did not show concern I gave up.

If what Irene wrote in the diaries was true then she was the kind of person mothers warned their children about when teaching them against vices. She came to the world too soon and adapted too fast; the speed of events she described in those detailed diaries would have been only possible in a movie. I would bet that she would get first prize in a reality show when describing the true meaning of vices. What was written inside there would have casted doubt in the mind of anyone who knew her age or the casual look on her face before she grabbed a cigarette. I would have doubted it myself were it not for hundreds of photos inside the album I had finished viewing. Her life was an industry whose raw materials came from ill motives deep within and accelerated by those in her life who had no information about the appearance and reality Meyer was talking about. The output went to the ready market which by some complex reason accepted the finished toxic products.

Irene's birthday coincided with April fool's day. She was a trickster who managed to juggle men like stones and blackmail them without a single incident of confrontation. Another unique thing with her birth was that she opened her eyes within two hours. The nurses wondered what was happening. She refused to suck her mother's breast and survived on bottle milk until she was able to eat solid food. All this was in detail in the notes column of her birthday. She was born in an abnormal way and lived an abnormal life.

She must have gone through the pages several times because some more important lines were underlined several times. She likened things she saw with what she thought. At one time she looked at a train which passed behind a slum where they lived and likened it to human life because it was so long that one would think its end can never be seen, and she thought its rusted body resembled the reality of the dilapidated life in her family. She described the irritating, loud siren it produced, which tore into people's ears, making them long for the time it would stop, whenever it approached where a road crossed the rails. It was a disturbance that seemed to remind everyone that people were not supposed to be happy all the time.

Born in a family of eight her life was a journey which saw her mother marry and divorce six men. They had lived in seven slums before they settled along Nairobi Mombasa highway, after which they went on their own. The first place she called home was Marsabit, barely a kilometre from a desert in northern Kenya. The disaster prone region from drought to floods and from starvation to thirst would have been only described as hell on earth, but Irene indicated in the short notes that it was the most beautiful place she had ever seen. The lifeless landscapes and the scorching sun which limited settlements made her feel wonderful. She described the sandy soils and the scanty thorn vegetation as the most fascinating things on the surface of the earth. She, however, admitted that she did not like seeing a lot of people. She saw them as restless as insect larvae in a latrine which did not succeed living forever, not even achieving it using their numbers. They were always in action to make or destroy for unending selfish gains that they did not acquire, but in the end died when options became limited like the larvae did when the water levels went low. Very few made it out of that pool to live a little longer. She boasted to be among them by attributing it to being wary of change in the most unobservable changes.

She described her mother as a disciplinarian who did not hesitate to pull their ears and rain slaps on the face of anyone she found doing something she did not like. She disappeared without saying where she was going when darkness fell and came back in the morning looking upset. The first thing she did was to look for mistakes and she rarely missed any. She would ask whose duty it was to sweep the house or question the quantity of sugar she left the previous day on the shelf. One of the things she never failed to remind anyone she was scolding was about their father's characteristics. They memorised what she said and abused each other whenever they disagreed but only if their mother was absent. Whenever she was on the receiving end her mother used to call her a porcupine. Her sisters giggled knowing it meant she was something ugly, like her father. I turned to look at the photo of a giant porcupine on the opposite wall. I had failed to understand when she wrote in the previous day's page that she styled her hair to look like quills of a porcupine, but it still looked lovely.

When her mother separated with her father she was just a young girl of five. That was the last time she saw him and the coastal town of Mombasa. He used to be a fisherman and providing for the large family was not easy. He was a drug user, but she insisted in the diary that she loved him. She called him a good father, who despite the fact that he did not lead an upright life, tried as much as he could to keep the family afloat. When he used to come home in the middle of the night he made sure he went to her room to make sure that she was sleeping well before he went to his bedroom. He brought her a teddy bear or a cowry shell from the beaches, and even when her mother complained that it was in the middle of the night he woke her up and gave her the gifts. He did not hate her four elder sisters but she could tell that they did not like him. She wrote in detail about the day when he took her out in the moonlight and described him as the most courageous father in the world when he took time to tell her about her failures and admitted that it would be difficult to be different but she needed to try. Two weeks after he divorced her mother, he was shot from behind at the harbour.

The turning point in Irene's life was when she discovered what her mother did for a living. She was tempted to search her lockable wardrobe, which was something they had grown not even thinking about. She found a gun and a book of various codes which had dates and most of them were ticked. There were various receipts of huge sums of banked money despite the fact that they lived in terrible poverty. That was when she discovered that her mother was a hit woman who killed for money. Neither she nor her siblings were in school and there were no signs that it would happen any time in the future. She woke up one cold morning and took to the streets, never to go back again. From what would not have been expected, she sent herself to school using means she did not describe in her journal. At one time she equated herself and people around her to the two ends of the alimentary canal: one side needed the other, but the other was independent.

The strong wind outside sent the curtain flying from the open window. Irene went and shut it slowly. Several doors and windows in the block banged, breaking and dismantling glass which fell to the floor and reduced to fragments. The students did not care about the breaking glass, because the maintenance department was to replace them first thing in the morning. They covered themselves more to protect themselves from the cold wind and the sound of the banging windows. Those whose clothes were on the lines went to take them to their rooms for safety. They did not bother to look for the ones which the wind managed to blow away with the pegs, along Thika Road, those disappeared before they touched the ground. Poverty and theft embraced each other like water percolating on loose sand. I could see street children picking pegs on the side of the road and stuffing them into their dirty pockets. They would then be washed and sold at a throw-away price somewhere on the black market. People lived in poverty and fear, anticipating the days which followed through guesswork. They exchanged bad intentions to make sure they saw the days that followed but above all there was life which was the only thing which never ceased to exist in that place.

Much as I still failed to know why Irene was always not in female company, I knew too well that it was not that she enjoyed masculine company. On one occasion, after her numerous affairs, she described men as lizards who spent so much time shifting places to regulate their temperature that it limited the time they were supposed to be foraging. It was another way of saying they preferred emotion over reason. I had unearthed the secret behind what she did and why, dating back from her childhood which recorded a series of disasters and tragedy. I did not spend time with psychology books for nothing, like my father always implied, and I knew what experiences in childhood did to people when they were adults, but at that time I was a journalist and not a psychologist therefore my work was to retrieve information and not act upon it. I did not know how she came to know it, but with a person like Irene I was not surprised either when she knew what I did and that was why she had allowed me access to her private information.

There were people whose life depended on other people's deaths, like Irene's mother. Some lied so that they could tell the truth like Irene, because a lie tasted like sugar and the truth tasted like soda ash. That was the world out there and then as darkness started falling, wary mothers warned children against playing away from the compounds. They would easily be turned into quick cash by child traffickers or into corpses by the speeding vehicles, which would not stop but go into hiding until everything was forgotten. Evil bordered the devil, and when one did not exist in a place the other took advantage. Shelter from darkness in houses shifted duty to family problems and conflicts caused by drunkenness and unfaithfulness of husbands, which were triggered by incompetence and high expectations of nagging wives who spent the day gossiping and comparing their households with those of their friends in the neighbourhood. The mothers fed children and herded them to their bedrooms thinking they were too young to see what was happening.

One of the lessons I learnt from my mother's death was that it was difficult to know how important something was unless one lost it. I remember when she used to tell me to work hard once I joined school so that I would get a good job and buy her sugar. Even when I sent some of the money I earned home for my sister's fees and family upkeep, I felt that I needed to reward my mother for the inspiration she gave me. There were people like me who felt the heavy salaries they earned did not have meanings in their lives because the people they loved most were not with them. Some people wished they had mothers, and the salaries they earned never added a meaning to their lives. I knew of people who worked hard but received burning disappointments in the end. I then learnt that one needed to spend time with the people they loved and tell them that they did in so many ways. Sometimes I bought my sister gifts and sent them home, not to add anything, but to show how much I cared.

The owl on the giant tree outside hooted with a vengeance as I turned the pages of the last diary. It was still the most feared bird in African communities, even at the height of civilisation. It was the scariest flying, living thing which carried a presage of disaster whenever it hooted. Primitive as it may have sounded, I think it somehow worked. I had seen with my own eyes people die in the neighbourhood after it landed on their roofs days or even hours prior. According to my grandfather it should have been hunted down and killed to tame the claws of death. It did work for his second wife after he killed it with an arrow when it landed on a wattle tree outside her house. When a second one landed on the roof while he was in the fields taking care of his animals, there was nobody at home. He died of breathing complications three days later. At the top of a giant tree at the college of foreign languages it would hoot as much as it wanted without a single person becoming interested.

Even when my hope was to give Russel the best life I never had I was aware that children were born every day as much as they died in Africa. Those stubborn to life joined the rest of the world to suffer and lead lives upside down then, became half-baked adults who were not different from their predecessors. They also gave birth to children who led struggling lives like themselves. It was an endless loop. Educating hungry people did not work, and the less educated they were the more they were prone to disease and poverty. Their life expectancy suffered deep cuts and they died before they lived. The few who made it looked like crocodiles, which had survived the dry season of a pool. Their survival was not enough because they got pulled down by dependent gravitational pulls. One-by-one they came tumbling down, overwhelmed by the number of mouths they had to feed and the number of holes in their pockets. If they failed to comply life would get lost. Sooner or later they became victims of their rescue and became equal and united in poverty and not against it. Death visited them one-by-one but strange as it sounded, life in the pool sprung again; how close or far from life and death depended on what happened in the pool.

In our country, Kenya, it was difficult for a person not to feel like they skipped a step in their lives. There was no situation which allowed people to stay in one place for long. Survival depended on movement. It is like the baby gazelle which is born and stands up to suck and walk within the same hour because the big cats and scavengers are always close behind. The breasts of the mothers they sucked were pulled from their mouths when they were sweetest because those born after them arrived too soon and needed the milk too. Looking at the lives the people led, one could easily tell that they had substituted their mother's teats with sucking thumbs, and theirs would be sad stories to their underfed families around fires. An elderly person was likely to talk about struggle and poverty when talking about his past; they usually shook their heads and creased their faces whenever they remembered. What I always failed to understand was why they did not pause in between their struggling lives to ask themselves whether they had made progress.

There was a man who called his son one day and told him that he was ripe for marriage. He went into a long story of their past and its struggles, telling him that he had risen from nothing to making a family that he referred to as his wealth. The son failed to understand because they grew up as a family of seven with one meal a day, and that was if they were lucky. Much as the enlightened world was busy with education and properly planned families, to the father, owning a family was the issue of concern and not what type of the family. The son rejected the request at that time but said that when time was right he would marry. The father insisted that he wanted to see his grandchild while he was alive. The son told him that he did not want to raise a family like the one he had grown up in but the father did not listen. The son went ahead and married and sired children, but the father did not die the way he had predicted. The added dependents added misery to the family and they could not be called wealthy anymore.

It was past midnight when I finished reading the last page of the diary, which she had described as collecting the pieces of her life. She had long slept on the couch and her breathing was heavy like that of a child. With her eyes closed she looked as harmless as a fly and she was like any other beautiful African girl. Even when she was asleep, part of her senses were active because she kept on whisking a mosquito away from her ear. She was different then from the girl smoking on the balcony and did not resemble the girl addicted to men in her room. She twisted her lips like a dreaming child and then swallowed. I tried to think about the young girl who spent her life shifting homes and places. The girl who expelled herself from her own family and took to the streets, then quite unexpectedly took herself to school and then wound up in a college of foreign languages. I could not imagine that person when I looked at Irene. I stood up to let blood flow to my legs. They had developed partial paralysis and were heavy. I piled the diaries on the table and left for my room.

Meyer was standing by the door talking to two girls who were in night dresses. They chuckled at whatever he was telling them, and I could tell they liked every bit of it. When he saw the room I was coming from he stopped to look at me and nodded his head longer than usual. The owl hooted again with a well-defined warning but I did not know at whom in particular. It must have stayed for a long time on that tree. In fact, longer than when the compound was a research institute. It had maintained its place on the ageless tree even when the compound had changed to a college of foreign languages with a large number of people. It had seen what happened on Thika road day and night and held vast information on what the people needed to do but decided to keep quiet. I did not know how much time it had stayed on that tree, but it must have been a long time. Whether there was agreement between its sound and what happened out there, it was difficult to tell.

After that day Irene agreed to an uncensored video interview. She was a courageous girl and I knew that was going in my favour. I was cautious though because I did not trust the reasons why she decided to tell the entire world how terrible her life had been. It sounded like a good beginning for the real story I had in mind. I wanted to set a proverb and its meaning to the ignorant people out there. I intended to dig out the true story and narrate it. I was determined to bring out what was always around but could not be seen in the limelight. Very few people understood that the people with horrible stories they read about and watched in the news were not very far away from themselves. There was that complex human tendency where people concentrated more on what others looked like than themselves. In the school of journalism there was a girl who had an abortion the previous week and was busy giggling and spreading word about another course mate who gave birth there a week after. In other words most people used their eyes more than their brains, and even when they did they failed to make interpretations of precision.

There was a teacher in a local primary school barely a kilometre from our home who used to come every morning to read a newspaper at the bridge where a vendor had erected a wooden structure for his business. With time the vendor erected benches and started to sell drinks to those who wanted to sit and read the papers. The teacher used to read and revise all papers but one thing even the vendor knew was that he walked away when he was done without buying anything. I did not know how his timetable was set because he never left the place before twelve o'clock. I used to buy a newspaper during weekends and sit to read it there when I was free or go to read at home. He was addicted to the job vacancies column and spent a lot of time with the detailed information. He would take a pen and record the details in his notebook moving his lips as he read. When one of my articles I wrote appeared on the papers I felt great because being a journalist was my dream career. I showed it to him with pride but he refused to accept it was me and argued that he had sent many articles before which were never published.

He was just like my father. He did not believe I would succeed in something he failed. I did not know it until one day when I told him that I wanted to put into use our idle seven acre land. He used to wake me up in the morning with our houseboy Tom during the dry season so we could set the bushes on fire to prevent snakes and rodents from multiplying. The land would then remain without use until the next dry season when we set the bushes and grass on fire again. Sometimes our thirty cattle would be left to roam on it to reduce the height of grass. When I told him I intended to do some farming he simply told me the piece of land was not fertile. I had accumulated heaps of organic manure with Tom from our animals which I intended to use for the purpose, but even when I told him of the plan I had in mind he refused. He told me that two sacks went on waste in two consecutive years when he had the same ideas as mine. He said that I would soon realise that the ideas I had formed in my head were as impossible as lighting a fire in a pool of water.

Much as I did not bother to tell my stepmother about it, there was a likelihood that it would not have made a difference. Even in the modern society I knew too well that my father was the chief executive when it came to management of family property and making decisions. Whenever desperation set in there was always that feeling that my mother would have given me a chance to do what I wanted, which affirmed itself in my mind with a strong adhesive of emotions and past events. I used to follow her to the garden to pluck kales for supper. I would try plucking fast like she did. Whenever she noticed I was interested in something, she did not put me off. Instead, she showed me how it was done. I would laugh my lungs off when she told me that she wanted me to grow up like a man so that I would work hard like an elephant breaking wood. Apart from my obligation of fulfilling my mother's dreams as the eldest son I had the responsibility of using available resources to raise the standards of our family, but I realised then it was not going to be as easy as I always thought.

I was on the last lap collecting information as I stood looking at what was happening at the side of the road while waiting for an entertainment at the hall in the early hours of a weekend evening. Young mothers and teenagers holding peeled sugarcane and other foodstuffs rushed to arriving vehicles from the capital at passenger dropping points and pleaded with those inside to buy their commodities, saying they were of high values at cheap prices. The tired passengers did not look at them twice but maintained their eyes on the door, yearning to put their feet on the ground to do other things they thought were more essential. Their minds were away calculating unyielding mathematics and their lives depended on hard decisions like lynching a chicken thief or pardoning him to continue stealing chicken. Two sheep tied to one tether wrapped their ropes around it by going round and around until their necks were pinned to it after a free roaming ram kept on harassing them by rapping their stomachs with its front limb and bleating obscenely.

The weather towards the upper side of the central highlands was calm and friendly with few white clouds above the sky not ready to turn dark any time soon. The rising population was quickly changing the local climate, altering the landscape which once stood as luxuriant forests and bushes. In the earlier years there was a Briton who read and heard stories about the beauty of the African country and flew in for the holidays to be part of what other people called a rare treasure in the world. Two hours after arrival he boarded a plane back to his country saying there was a very close similarity between the people and the animals he saw. He however said that he would have preferred to come as a researcher in anthropology and evolution not as a tourist on a holiday. That might have still been in memories of foreign hatred but even the homeless were aware that they needed each other when weekends approached for a common purpose they would call happiness. School children played close to vegetable vendors in excitement, glad they had a break from books until the following week on Monday.

Weekends were recipes for celebratory moods and chaos when bosses had a difficult time restraining their worker's minds. From the early hours of the afternoon all of them were on their watches. They were days when family related conflicts materialised and men woke up the days that followed breaking mirrors on seeing their swollen faces and missing teeth. Even the dumbest police officer loved to be on duty that day to collect bribes double his salary from the free roaming night lovers. All roads led to specific places and whenever people ate and drank more than they could pay for, they staged fights so that they could get away in the confusion. At Mark's, the administration constantly improved entertainment in an attempt to tie students inside, but they still preferred to go out. They stuck around playing indoor games then boarded vehicles to attend expensive dates in the capital and did not come back until Monday morning. Quite a number who were broke remained behind chewing stimulants and drinking cheap liquor after which they narrated drunken stories to pass the night.

It was easy to tell that students were happy together dancing that night and whispering lies to each other that they knew were not true, but they still loved them. Somewhere else, different things were happening behind their back, difficult to believe and illogical to accept. I investigated and caught on camera a girl who had sex with six different people that night. To me it was tragedy while to many others it did not happen. I was aware that as a young adult I was too careful, which limited my happiness or what others called fun in youth. The parent instinct in me played a role and my career made me learn, but above all my conscience would not have led me to think otherwise and I was glad. When one learnt and thought about everything which was happening out there it was difficult to smile, except in anger.

After the shocking witness I gathered that night, for the first time I felt like sharing what I had in mind with someone in a friendly conversation. Meyer might have had his downs, but I knew that he was a good listener and gave anyone time to talk about anything they wanted to. Given that my role was to gather information and give out recommendations without acting upon them, I felt like bending that rule a little that morning, when I left for the room from the entertainment hall, by telling Meyer that his lifestyle with many girls was not one of the best. When I reached the room I found him sleeping with the same girl I had caught on camera the previous night. Instead of dropping on my bed to catch some sleep, I went to stay to the balcony. The compound looked vacated then with the night lovers nursing mistakes and hangovers in their sleep to forget about what they did the previous night. A few minutes later I saw the girl leave. The owl broke into a tired hooting that was long but defined.

Chapter Four

Tracy brought me a fully signed letter from the Indian professor Nairit Aniruddha that said that I had been appointed the secretary general of the students mentoring programme. Professor Nairit or 'the kilogramme' as his students called him, was the head of department in Italian and spoke nine languages. Even when I was a regular attendant of the mentoring programme I did not understand why he decided to assign me such a committing job without my consent. It then occurred to me that he was a dictator like his students accused him of being. I assisted him even when I was not called upon but surprising me with an appointment was the last thing I had expected. The programme, which was initiated and chaired by him, was an addition to the sterile guidance counselling building whose workers reported every morning to get bored and wait for the end of the month. It almost looked like they were being paid for getting bored. I never saw a student step into that room and I suppose it was the most stressful job anyone would have been given. As may have been expected under the leadership of someone like Professor Nairit, the mentoring programme was poorly attended but it was slowly picking up because students attended it when they did not have anything to do.

Professor Nairit's nickname came to existence when one day he was harassed by stray dogs. That was the time everyone realised he was not as fierce as he made everyone believe. He was an addict of goat meat and it was said that meat was always available in his meal. He usually bought it from the college butchery claiming it was the only place he trusted. In fact, Professor Nairit did not do his shopping anywhere. When the dogs were looking for edibles, they sniffed the meat and they confronted him. He froze where he was standing. He calculated the distance to the car and decided it was too far away. As they came closer, barking, he started moving backward step-by-step until he broke into a run. Realising he was a coward, the dogs went for him. One hand was holding the meat in the air while the other supported his old back. He kept on shouting "my whole kilogramme of meat!" And then narrowed the words as the dogs decreased distance until he was just shouting "Kilogramme!" When he tripped and fell the dogs took his meat and left. He cursed and swore when security men arrived and said that they would pay for damages. I did not know whether he became serious with what he said or if he was compensated.

For the time I had attended the programme, I realised that anyone who was good in separating the message from the speaker would have seen that Nairit had great points in his long speeches. He had a weakness though when it came to taming his anger. Students made fun of him when they realised it. He would slap his thighs and swear caressing his long nose which looked like the trigger of a giant gun. Such a case happened one day when he carelessly called someone a fowl, whose cell phone started ringing in the middle of his speech. He went on describing him as a bird with a big body but a very small head. Phones started ringing from every corner as laughter greeted him. His attempts to calm the situation were drowned by shouts and even more laughter. He collected his books and called it a day. He had numerous degrees from Britain and the United States but for all the education they gave him they forgot to teach him about summary. He would tear into a detailed speech and wander away from the points until someone reminded him that time had elapsed. He should have gone for orientation with Mrs. Fabiano. She understood many things about us and maybe he would have stopped stressing himself with a learning approach which would never work as long as he was on African soil.

After considering many things, I rejected Nairit's appointment. I wrote him a letter explaining that I was not showing him disrespect but I had other inevitable commitments which needed me too. In other words, I was sending him a message that he needed to consult people before giving them such sensitive assignments which called for commitment even in his unique style of leadership. He might have got away with the way he dealt with everyone but I was sure he did not know how to deal with me. After he received my rejection letter he became mad and went to complain to Mrs. Fabiano. She called me that afternoon and we talked in great detail. When she failed to convince me to accept the job she said she would talk to professor Nairit about it. Nevertheless, I did not stop attending the mentoring programme. I had different reasons as to why I was interested in the programme, more than the assumption of dedication like the likes of Nairit took it to be.

The people for whom the mentoring programme had been set up for, like Irene and Meyer, did not attend it, but as the saying goes, "the productive animals receive the most supplements and the less productive ones can consume the remnants." Sometimes I helped carry Nairit's books to his office if he did not come with his car. The first day I went with him I was stunned when he inspected the lock and the door before he touched it. When he opened, he looked inside the office to make sure everything was intact as if he was taking precautions of a bomb threat before he let anyone in. He did the same thing to his car, or preferably, he parked it where he would see it while teaching. He would be seen walking around it with his potbelly and dragging his left leg which looked shorter. Whenever he took students for an academic tour, he usually slept in the temple because it was the only place he trusted. He was a complex person far away from the homeless people who snored in the street pavements where vehicles were speeding and hooting.

When the *Worldreach* television network tore the air waves with the special edition *Distance Between Life and Death* that I had compiled about the double lives in college, the people were shocked but soon rubbished it as fiction right to the college premises where I sat watching the news and listening to views. I was not surprised but at the same time I was not moved. My role was unearthing the truth and not to convince people who lived with it that it was real. It was always human tendency to lie to oneself about something, but it did not take long before a lie turned into a consequence of regret. There was a story of a father who defended his wicked son. He claimed that he was not a thief and ignored any allegations which connected him to theft. One day the son stole from him, and that was when he realised how deep the issue had gone. In an attempt to correct him he threatened to set him up to the authorities for a jail term of several years. The son took the threat seriously and strangled him to death. Even when he shouted apologies for his ignorance; all that time no one heard him.

Life goes on. From the streets of the city to the apartments of the rich, and from the slums of poverty to the remote areas of the primitive. I saw that from the window of an apartment I rented in the capital for security, which was one of the major rules of a sensitive coverage. The red and yellow lights down there hid people's faces and identifications but it did not hide what they were doing. The people retiring from their jobs were headed to various houses of entertainment so that they would report at their desks early the day that followed to make rich men richer. Merchants were set for the business hours and made sure their clients did not miss anything which would alter their profits that night. People crossed the streets in pairs to various places of entertainment as school girls roamed with strangers from one cabaret to the other easily coaxed by money. Charcoal burners were there on time roasting maize and making anything that went with the weather as hawkers and fraudsters mixed with drug traffickers in the evening traffic confusion. The water under the bridge flowed silently without suspicion because those who played the games had extra senses for cops.

It was life far away from Thika Road for school children with patched uniforms who boarded passenger buses to school for free when businesses were down. They sat in similar classes with those who were driven to school by family vehicles, but even when they were optimistic that they would make it, doubt became their major obstacle. They would be seen shivering at the sides of the road early in the morning with moody faces which were smeared with cooking fat to prevent them from drying. Their mothers just sent them to the passenger picking points after eating the previous night's leftovers because money for breakfast would be saved for both a cheap lunch and supper so that few shillings could also be saved for rent, and to avoid quarrels about family expenditure with their jobless fathers at the end of the month. They would look different standing there with non-school pullovers compared to their smart schoolmates whose hands were held by maidens. Wicked minded people took advantage of girls especially after darkness found them still waiting in panic at the picking points.

They might not have lived on bread at all but they existed anyway. They were numerous behind Mark's where slums easily sprung with people who came from near and far with entrepreneurial minds, hoping to take advantage of the college to improve their living standards. The businesses sprung faster than they could establish. Competition set in, forcing the owners to subsidize the prices to stand chances. As a result the profits went down and down and finally counting of losses began. More people attracted by the activities poured in hoping to find some employment if at all they would not employ themselves. With time, good intentions sired bad ideas, as a result of frustrations and insecurity intervened. Contrary as per the expectations in their minds, when they arrived the living standards either remained the same or worsened. Their situation called for bigger minds and it remained as the only chance of survival. The aftermath could be seen as the children of the people inherited the poverty and the cycle would begin again. It went on forever.

At the time I was wondering what it felt like living on guesswork, Tracy was preparing to carry out a research on problems women were going through around Mark's University College. She worked part-time at a women empowerment programme firm in the capital. I did not refuse when she requested me to help her. It was difficult to turn her down because she knew how to word a request, and anyone who knew her would have agreed that she did not just request anybody. One thing that was always part of me was casting doubt, and despite the fact that philosophy endorsed it in any creativity it was with me long before I touched any books. Tracy's way of life was different from one or two things I knew about women. Strange as it sounded, she knew that I doubted which would have easily led to a refusal and she took time to explain. I understood that at times I overrated myself and what I expected about other people was too much but I failed to think or behave otherwise. I remember Russel's mother saying when we were young that I was the scariest person to spend time with for anyone who did not know me well because it was difficult to know what was going on in my mind.

We left to the streets of the slum armed with questionnaires but if the answers we were going to get would have been like those of my shoe shiner then the accuracy of the information would have formed question marks in my mind. The man in his early sixties had spent half of his life polishing shoes and selling newspapers on the same spot. He liked seeing me because he knew I paid without bargaining. He would then tear into stories about the place and did not mind when nobody was listening. All he needed was someone to be around. His chief customers were elderly people who came to share stories, which did not help them beyond passing time. As a reporter, experience had taught me that if anyone liked talking about his past then his present and future were not working for him. Despite claiming that he had put his four children in high school among other expenses with a shoe shining and newspaper business, I immediately doubted it in my mind unless he had other alternative means. He had a badly patched pair of shoes which were over polished from cleaning polish container sides on them before discarding. He also had an old blue coat with a faded newspaper name at the back which he never took off. The women selling vegetables beside him said it had special magic for attracting business, and he seemed to like it because it did not upset him.

It did not take long to realise the alternative activities the people ventured into when life proved hard. They would handle it like the pregnant woman who stood by a charcoal burner on which maize was boiling. It was as if her pregnancy had happened to illustrate her load of problems. It protruded infront of her like a giant balloon threatening to burst at the slightest bruise. She stood legs asunder eating maize from a cob she held with protruded eyes like a grazing cow wary of thorns. Her feet supported her weight somehow with toes spread wide apart on the ground with mud in between like a distorted garden fork. Her die hard child, which had refused to eat the maize in the cold morning, clung to her dress watching the world while sucking on its thumb. She was upset and refused to talk until Tracy persuaded her, and when she did it was always the same old story of men running away from their families because they did not want to watch them starve to death. Her husband left her one morning when she was pregnant to look for a job and never came back.

Poor people were likely to turn violent for different reasons but all their reasons always translated into protest against oppression. It was easy to think their misfortunes were caused by people above their economic class who they claimed were obstacles to their rising. As it was the case, in slums they became united in poverty and felt more related than other businessmen who settled in places altering the prices of basic commodities the way they felt like. When a vehicle carrying poultry feeds knocked a man who was trying to cross the road on his bicycle, weird looking characters and idlers rushed to the scene with biased compensation demands. They shouted at the vehicle driver telling him how people with money did not treat them as human beings. The driver maintained a casual look and took the bicycle owner aside and they negotiated. Keen eyes were glued to their direction and when hands were exchanged they knew the driver had given him something. When the vehicle pulled away they boasted about what a force they were made of and demanded a share for their persuasive powers. When they got it they bought cigarettes and chewing gums.

There was a time I asked children what they thought kept the distance between life and death. They gave a variety of answers, but most of them agreed it was food. As much as those bright children reasoned out and gave me prudent answers, there was a strong sense of innocence about the world and all evils they could not imagine existed at least for that time. They were strangers in their own world until they grew up and discovered they had no idea what the real distance was. As we collected information with Tracy from one person to the other, I saw the endless activities of restless men and women walking up and down the dirty streets to do something so that they would be able to put food on the table to keep the distance. Theirs was different from those others I saw in the capital because they operated from hand to mouth, while those in the capital operated from pocket to hand. While they slept late and woke up early to make sure their families did not sleep hungry, the people in the capital worked hard to improve their lives and those of their families.

The aftermath of hungry children came to haunt the families like marauding ghosts when they stopped going to school and instead chipped in to help their struggling parents earn a living. The parents did not ask because they understood and I saw quite a number playing with balls made of waste paper and silk strings along the streets while their frustrated mothers stood at fruit stalls without customers. The previous month, a woman put a knife she chopped vegetables with in the eye of a scrap metal dealer when he joked that she was waiting to make profit out of items worth less than fifty shillings. The people were overwhelmed by the action rather than the cause and they did what they usually did in such situation by beating up the woman. The man became a hero of sympathy at that time, but days after they started making open jokes about how weak he was to an extent of not stopping a knife in his eye socket from a woman. They did not report to the authorities because there was always the fear of spending money which was what they did not have. Days after the woman was found dead in a sewer trench that emptied its contents in the river to the south.

They might have spent most of their times to get something for their stomach but they hoped than one day they would rise up like those who sat behind steering wheels, with extended stomachs, along Thika Road. For all the time they were idle their minds were wandering far away from the world of realities which was the biggest consolation at least for that time. Their thinking was wide and their hopes were undying but the facts were few. That would only be interpreted when one looked at their dry mouths and sunken eyes that did not blink and were not aware of themselves or their children who kept on crying beside them because they were hungry. Their torn clothes which stood the test of time and worn out cheap sandals made people get out of their way wherever they went because they did not know what they expected. I saw such a case sitting on a stone near a food house made up of old corroded iron sheets. He was a young man in his mid-twenties who was modified by life to look like an old man of seventy. His fleshless cheeks stuck out, covered by withered skin on which a brown beard stuck out like crops with limited nutrients. He was waiting to see if someone for splitting firewood would be required and puffing on a cigarette just to keep himself busy.

We heard terrible stories from women who were trying to turn their lives around and some of them were optimistic that it would happen one day. What was interesting in all those revelations was that whenever they felt they would not be able to improve the families themselves, they strongly believed their children would. There was a woman who lit her face with a smile like a flicker of light in a storm when she said her three children were blessings. The youngest was crawling and she was pregnant then. Their mouths were shining and greasy from eating potato chips she was making and selling in the open. She understood the importance of education and believed she would find a way of sending her children to school. I had a strong reason to doubt because the eldest child was supposed to have started schooling about two years before. Young as she was, she peeled the potatoes and skillfully chopped them into sizeable pieces which indicated that she had done that for quite some time. The father of the children was out there looking for an alternative source of income and she did not know where he was until he came back deep in the night to narrate where he had been.

Even when the basis of improvement for micro-businesses and subsistence consumption was increasing the income, I was convinced that it was difficult to improve what one did not have. It was like treating the symptoms of a disease and not the disease, or trying to put out the fire from the tongues and not the base. There were various self-help groups out there which soon collapsed because as it was soon realised that there were more expenditures than savings. The people tried to live normally by giving themselves entertainment. Slum gangs used the houses as hideouts for robberies and fraud against those who had no information about what happened there. Late at night loud music would be heard coming from secluded cheap houses of entertainment. People narrated drunken stories about their past and those they knew who had made it, as well as how they planned to improve themselves. At least for that time they were people united in poverty, but after daybreak they were met with the daily reality of stagnating in square one or below.

Far away yet so near from the struggling adults there was quite a different family in that place. It was the family of homeless children in the streets. Whenever Tracy saw suffering children she wept openly and took a long time to recover from it. Their lives were like those scavenger birds which operated on luck. They sniffed glue bottles to disturb their minds a little because it was impossible to face the conditions out there day and night. They witnessed what happened there day and night, like the owl on the giant tree outside my hostel. They also decided not to migrate and stood the test of time in life or death in the streets. Their only respect came from the marabou storks which flew away when they saw them from piles of rotting materials down at the illegal dumping site. They were abandoned children left in the streets to die. Some of them did not even remember how they happened in the streets. They waited to scavenge for food scraps in the streets which were rare because the food house owners collected and sold them to poultry keepers.

I turned my eyes from the blaring sun and the stench of the garbage to the capital shining beyond the hills. Maybe a parent to who one of those children belonged was somewhere there. There was a possibility because some of the women told us they were abandoned by fathers of their children and decided to settle in the slums. Some admitted having abandoned their children elsewhere because the only thing life promised was death. There were many others who left their children in the streets because they came into being as a mistake who were then condemned to suffer. That was the category which rode on high-class levels and made merry in that shining city of secrecy and blackmail. It was difficult to understand why people added children to the streets day after day. Some men came from far and enticed desperate girls with goodies, like the pregnant girl in a school uniform I talked to who was selling a handful of kales and did not seem to care by laughing and joking about the innocent life which was growing in her. From what I gathered that was likely to be another street life in the near future.

Mrs. Fabiano said something in class one day but I could see that even when she was serious there was some information she wanted to gather. She said during a joke that in Africa, women and children were more related but men were on their own. That was after a research the previous week showed that a high percentage of men in the country did not know the exact birthdays of their children. The men rubbished the report in the media accusing those who had carried out the research of bias. When members of the media, carried out their interviews the results were not different. We kept on laughing watching television because when men were asked what the ages of their children were, they had to add them up using fingers. My father was a victim in that research and I had not taken time before to think it happened elsewhere. The class went into a long argument while she patiently listened to their views. At long last even boys agreed but did not say so.

After we gathered enough we entered one of the hotels, not because we wanted to eat but to have a look at what happened inside there. Hungry and angry people shouted at those serving them and yelled abuses when their orders were delayed, telling them there were many hotels around while opening wallets that were marks down. They were the same people who left starving families back home claiming they were running away from nagging wives and children who made incessant demands. They spent hours looking for jobs and putting in their mouth what their hands touched then snuck back to their homes when it was dark for the night and disappeared before the cock crowed, leaving the children to their wives who prepared them for school.

There were several reasons as to why many preachers emerged in such a place. First, it was the only job which did not call for paying taxes therefore free of harassment from the city council. Second, there were very few people who dared question religious matters and therefore the preachers would set up any doctrines they felt like. Third, hope and fear were two principles that went hand-in-hand with poverty which engulfed the place like couch grass in the rainy season. Their strong voices penetrated the hotel walls from close range. When I looked out of the window there were two men who were preaching barely fifteen metres apart but each had his own congregation. They preached the message of giving no matter where they started from. When competition became stiff they fought over space and exchanged bitter words. One thing I knew they never missed in such a place was an audience, and I could see quite a number with crossed arms listening and comparing.

There was one such individual that I sent away from our house when I was barely fifteen. My step mother used to entertain a number by making them food every time they came, so that they got used to the routine that they would not leave unless they had eaten. They did not mind waiting for food to cook while quoting the Bible, making prophesies and praying a number of times. Most of them had dropped out of school years back and said they were heeding to a religious call. My stepmother was a serious person when it came to matters related to religion and I had no peace with preparing meals and bringing green bananas from the farm for them. One day, while my stepmother was away from home, a man who had sent his wife away months before came while I was reading a book in the dining room. Whenever there was nobody at home I kept the door locked from the inside.

When he knocked instead of opening the door I opened the window. When he saw he was not welcome after I told him there was nobody at home he decided to preach from the window and started opening his bag. I simply told him I was busy and went back to my book. He went ahead and demanded food explaining that it is what people did wherever they went. I told him to go home and work on his farm then closed the window. He said a few threatening words before he clicked and went away. Coincidentally the previous week our Sunday school teacher had warned me that religious issues were never questioned after I stupidly asked if God really took the money we contributed. She reported it to my stepmother who threatened to starve me if I did not behave. My father never asked anything about issues which did not affect him directly. He listened unconsciously sipping on his coffee while my stepmother counted one mistake after the other, and when the storm calmed down he asked about different things.

When I did not know Tracy well, I cracked a careless joke which forced me to apologise moments later after I realised how much harm it had done to her. I knew how emotions affected women when it came to talking about suffering children, but I did not know that a simple joke would have produced the same result. She started talking about how she dreamt all her life to establish a children's home which would provide opportunities for a promising life and nurture wasted talents. That was when I said that such a move was likely to encourage children in the streets. I did not know then that Tracy spent almost all her child hood in the streets until a well-wisher picked her up and gave her an opportunity to a have a place to call home. I also did not know that what she said was a lifelong dream which she would not have let anything take away from her. She looked at me for a moment and turned her eyes away. Her face changed like disappearance of sunlight before a storm. I learnt that not all jokes were welcome in any situations.

Tracy's dream made me remember Aristotle's framed word on the wall of our living room. The frame was there before I was born and had not been shifted like other picture frames. They were the words of Albert Einstein which said that *only a life lived for others is a life worth living.* There were many people out there with beautiful dreams like Tracy but their results depended on how one would have been immune to pressures which killed them every day. That was what shaped our lives for better or for worse. It was nice to remember about friends when we were still young and the way we talked about what we wanted in the future, but it was sad to see that very few lived up to their dreams. They were sweet memories of good friends, some who had died. I remembered the times we used to call girls 'sheep' after the famous childhood game where a boy was blindfolded and would look for a girl who was not. She would then hide behind him or in front of him as he kept on stretching his arms to grab her. He would then repeatedly shout "My sheep!"And the girl would reply with bleating and change position.

I was not fortunate enough to find someone to tell me when I was young that speaking alone was not becoming when climbing the ladder of success, but I was lucky that it manifested itself in me as if I had seen it work. To make it from the kind of school I joined after elementary school, I needed someone who would think about making something out of nothing. It was located in the middle of thick trees and farms. It was not visible from a distance, nor was it accessible except by any means of transport other than by bicycle and by foot. Those others who studied in towns used to tell us we were learning in a 'bush' school when they came for holidays. Anyone who was brought up in the capital would have thought it was a practical impossibility to learn in such a place. Walking to school along the village path one would meet villagers with machetes who were up early to stare at people who walked in different directions. It was easy to get ambushed along the way, and hearing an exchange of threatening words from people who had a mentality of conflicts was common. Four school boys who threatened the former school principal after he punished them waited for the principal down the river and fed him cow dung.

One of the most important things I learnt when schooling at my home place was that it was not something good at all to talk about failure on the track to success. That was the only situation I knew "speaking" translated to "becoming" I do not know how it started but I remember a talk which was initiated during free time, where boys asked each other what mark one would leave behind if death visited at that time. They asked each other in turn and skipped me because they knew I rarely reserved comments which would impress them in such discussions. With time they all agreed it was children. They shared many things and that was the reason they always sat behind in class. In other words, they were looking for something they were good at apart from schoolwork. One thing I did when a friend was drowning was to learn about swimming and I did that by keeping quiet. They manifested the casual talk in their minds then went practical by impregnating girls in the village.

They dropped out of school to marry because as they argued, married people were accorded respect and dignity. They sired children faster than they could handle but death did not visit them as soon as they thought. They were the same people who became heavy burdens to their families and their brothers and sisters who worked hard to get to great heights by becoming gravitational pulls in their achievements. Their hand-to-mouth families competed for shopping meant for parents, which their brothers and sisters sent from towns where they worked at the end of the month. They were the same people whose wives looked like old gazelles at young ages because they had to go from one farm to the other to pick tea and form casual labours to get money for their children's food to make them see the day that followed. They would be seen associating themselves with sons of men who came back to the villages driving fancied vehicles so that they would pull a fifty or a hundred shillings from them.

Afterwards they made impromptu visits to distant relatives in town and lodged there claiming to look for jobs for which they did not have qualifications. Pressures of living costs increased because they became dependents in families that were comfortable before they came and disagreements on expenditures arose threatening to break the families apart. They would be sent back to the village or they would decide to settle in slums to look for low-paying jobs. They became determined to do anything so long as it paid and hoped to make money to help their families, which time indicated that it would not translate into expectations. Soon their families back at home joined them and their dreams died one by one as the conditions became unbearable. They finally abandoned their wives and children then went to settle elsewhere having run short of options. Their children found no other options than to flow into the streets to survive on mystery if at all they were lucky. It repeated itself on and on and that was why children were always in the streets.

Chapter Five

The best way to get along with professor Nairit when he was not in a good mood was by pretending you were interested in what he was saying. By so doing, he felt appreciated and respected which made him spend less time talking. After he finished telling me about what disgusted him in the traffic jam, he introduced me to his son Haamid who had arrived from Mumbai that morning. Haamid was a cool and patient person who let his father speak as much as he wanted. He had graduated from the school of law and had crossed over to the continent to see new people and learn new languages while waiting for opportunities. Nairit wanted me to show him around while he went to attend his lessons. He gave Haamid his credit card and wished us a nice time.

"He is a good chap," he told me.

"Tell him to keep a distance with girls around this place," he added biting his lip.

I laughed as he turned to go.

Haamid was a big contrast to his father, which would have easily told someone that they did not spend a lot of time together. He was positive about other people and understood what they did even when they did it wrongly. One thing I noticed though for that short time I saw father and son together was that he was not strict to him the way he was with everyone else. He talked to him casually and even gave him his credit card and one of his cars, something anybody who knew professor Nairit well would have called unusual. We went around the college so he could see what it looked like and then went to my room and spent the rest of the time there before lunch. He had a strong sense of social experience because he knew what to speak about and when. His father was right about keeping distance even when he had said it as a joke because those sniffing girls had started peeping from their windows to see what the new fish in the net looked like.

We left for the capital. After Mrs. Fabiano's lecture, there were no more lessons in the afternoon. Haamid wanted me to show him a cricket playground. He was an addict of the game and had represented his county while he was studying there. Haamid's birth came at a time when his parents were on the verge of a breakup. They at last obtained a tinge of happiness and would smile even after twenty five-years of marriage. The happiness did not last. A few years later his parents divorced when he was still young and his mother was granted custody. He had lived with her until she died when he was about to join law school. For all the time he lived with his mother, professor Nairit visited him regularly and funded his upkeep. He loved both of them as his parents and did not take sides when he made decisions. The aging professor who was in his mid-seventies then guarded him jealously because he was the only thing that signified that he once existed.

The major difference, which put me at a disadvantage of collective thinking, was what I really thought life was. It was not easy for someone to choose the lifestyle I chose without looking different or not having many friends. I always felt like a bee left behind by a migrating swarm, which would not have made honey on its own, therefore, saw no point of collecting nectar. What came defining itself in my toughest principle was that it did not mean the bee would not sting. There were other bees like professor Nairit who had been left behind by time factor and were trying to collect nectar by telling the world what did not interest them. Feeling alone in the whole world sent someone against it. Their voices were not given ears, and their causes were taken for granted. They existed almost functionless to other people, like planets which revolved without causing seasons. The change of times swallowed their values like a sea tide storming an island and their points were only reserved in historical books and journals years after them. There was no doubt that they would be respected and put in the memories of the few who cared about the great past, but it would sound like a story which would never apply in the years of those to whom it was narrated. Another history maker would emerge and the same process would start again. It was like racing for hours to look behind and find no distance covered.

The people were patient to wait for rain so that they could see where roofs were leaking. It was similar from a higher learning institution like Mark's to the free roaming world out there, and Haamid understood all those things. Within hours after landing in a foreign continent, he fit in like a key in the right padlock. He would laugh or smile and sometimes joke with strangers but understood his limits quite well with an experience no one would have thought of. I was one of the strangers but quite different because he in particular did not find me amusing. His approach was different but it worked well with him by turning a deaf ear and a blind eye to what was happening out there. I understood. He was not a journalist and as a servant of his field of specialisation, people would shout from Khartoom to Johannesburg or trample the planet the way they wanted, so long as they did not break the law.

Some people were controversial against their expectations like me, and their opinion always fell where there was no majority like my mother, Uwimana. Some of it was a decision while the rest would have been a series of wavy events beyond salvation. My earliest teacher, who was my mother, made me understand all that. She was born as the second daughter of the old man Ingabire Ishimwe in Kigali, Rwanda, sixteen years after her elder sister. She became the only survivor of the ill-fated family, which perished in an accident when she was just fifteen. She had found her way all the way from the capital to Bukavu to look for a living. She met my father, there who was at the time working for an environmental conservation firm. They had travelled all the way from Nairobi to carry out a research on the famous Lake Kivu. Three years later they got married and came to settle deep in the south. She was my grandfather's favourite daughter-in-law because she worked hard on the farm and made sure that he was not hungry as long as she was around.

There was a dance my grandfather used to perform in my mother's praise at the first taste of the season's harvest. It was a culture there that the eldest man in the family tasted the harvest first. It had faded with time when communal purposes lost meaning because people were then interested in different things. He used to play his old traditional drum and then shake his old shoulders forwards and backwards. We would then perform a dance by going around and around in a circle while he played the instrument. He had a special song for my mother and whenever he started singing it my mother went inside the circle and danced by twisting her waist and shaking her shoulders. The others joined her one-by-one and the circle would break. When the dance was over my grandfather slaughtered a goat and the women prepared dishes in the open fires around his compound. The feast would continue until people were tired late in the night. It was a wonderful occasion and I longed for it, particularly the dance to the song which praised my mother.

One thing even my father did not know was that I spoke fluent Kinyarwanda. My mother used to teach me a great deal of it when he was away, and we would talk while she was preparing meals or working in the garden. She did not use it whenever my father was around or other visitors. One day I asked her why she did not like us using the language while other people were there. She told me it was because they would not understand the language but when I insisted that we teach father as well, she took time to answer and looked around before she did. She whispered to me that father did not like the language. She, however said, that it made her feel like a stranger. It occurred to me then that what he did not know meant he also did not want me to know. I had learnt that whatever my mother cautioned me about was always serious. I did not know how it happened but my grandfather knew how to speak the language and liked it. I snuck out during free times to talk with him in his hut, and I would then feel out of place in my country of birth.

As far as Tracy was concerned, life meant becoming a servant of the less fortunate. She was specific though, and children touched her more. The trend of the future was easily shaped by early observations and actions which followed in the mind and depended on various interpretations. For Tracy, it was children, but for me, it was their mothers. I believed that whenever one wanted to clean a river well, the best place he would have started with was the source. I reached the conclusion because of what I witnessed as a boy who grew up in the bushy village. Our home was situated some metres to the river and beside the river there was a spring inside the trees which never went dry, rain or sunshine. Anyone who lived around that place did not see the need for piped water. The only people who did were those who came from towns to settle on the pieces of land they bought. The people saw them as lazy individuals who would not carry a bucket of water from the river a few metres away and took them as rich people who had money to waste. Their housekeepers went to the river only when the water pumps stopped functioning or their water tanks went empty, which was not rare.

I used to go to the river with a story book and sit inside ferns reading while the river roared downstream shaping its channel the way it wanted. The amount of water increased during the rainy seasons and then it would get scary, shaking vegetation along the banks as the water moved down the slope. There were numerous birds living inside those gum trees which grew close and big with a lot of rain. Our trees were many and grew close because they all established after we planted them close thinking only few would survive. A number of hare existed in the trees and children loved to go hunting for sport and food. Types of swampy grass and water plants grew close to the river when it became muddy in the rainy season, and then they would disappear during dry season. I read as many stories as my concentration would take, then watch the flowing mass of water or dragon flies dipping their tails in the water when I was tired. Were it that I had opted out of being a journalist, sometimes I thought of studying natural science.

When the sun penetrated the canopies and the heat found its way to the ground, I walked close to the channel and sat on the bank with my legs inside the water. I then enjoyed looking at birds diving and washing their wings from the rocks of numerous tributaries which fed the river. My father had warned me against risking being bitten by a snake but that did not prevent me from going to the river. I was not afraid of snakes, and besides, the trees were full of green mambas which were not poisonous. For all the time I had been to the river I had never seen any other. The poisonous ones were said to be inside the water but no one testified that he had seen one. I knew that was a precaution which protective mothers used to scare children from going close to the river. There was the story of the second wife of my grandfather who found a python coiled inside an empty water pot where she kept sugar in her kitchen. She was then newly married and never returned to the kitchen until a new one was built for her.

Even when I was not afraid of snakes there was another group of reptiles I was afraid of. It was the world of chameleons. My baby sister used to wonder why I would be brave to reptiles which were harmful and a coward of those which were harmless. To me, a chameleon was the ugliest thing I ever knew, especially the old ones which had oversized skins making them wrinkled at the neck. While my baby sister was wondering about my relationship with chameleons, I was wondering how a living thing would change colour and make slow movements as if it was afraid of using its energy. Then there was that fast grip on something it managed on two fingers with its limbs and the long tongue it lashed out every time it was on its prey. I never went near any place I saw one. Whenever there was one near the cattle shades I attempted to remove it then before our houseboy Tom would discover and chase me around the compound with it.

I used to be oversensitive when working on our farm. I was wary of bending twigs when digging because one would have easily crawled onto my back without me noticing. That was days after my shirt became heavy on one side and I asked Tom to look at my back, the first time since we started working at the farm. We did not talk that morning because he wore my jacket to visit his girlfriend the day before. I threatened to beat him up if he did not stick to his own clothes. Instead of telling me what the problem was he gave himself a victorious smile and told my sister to have a look. She started screaming which was an indication that whatever she saw would not have pleased me. I did not then need to be told what it was and all I remember was that I went mad running the whole field with my back bent forward to avoid contact while calling for help at the top of my lungs, until the neighbours came to my rescue. They then found the opportunity to call me names. Tom kept on laughing throughout the day whenever he saw me.

There were numerous chameleons in the trees down by the river, but I still preferred spending time there. It was the only place where I felt my mind was at peace. It was a safe place, not from physical attacks but from noisy villagers and the constant gossips I had grown up with. I was aware that I did many things my age mates did not do and achieved what they failed which generated a conflict of interest. I did not share gulps of traditional wine in the bushes with them nor did I wait to ambush village maidens when going to the river like they did. They tended to avoid me, having felt if I was not for something then I was against, it so we became enemies without saying it. They openly called me "the pope" then giggled uniformly like balloons inflated with air of foolishness. When I was given an award for taking care of Russel and being the best student overall in the province by the Portuguese father Alberto Agostinho, who was going back to his country after thirty-five years of charity missions in the country, very few people opened their mouths to say "congratulation". I did not understand why I always suffered from the guilt of difference.

Father Alberto inspired me in so many ways. He was the one who made me want to write and speak Portuguese since I was a child. He was as harmless as a butterfly and was always smiling to anybody who met him. Many people used to feel Sunday school was not complete without his sermon. He would walk during break time from one group of children to the other wiping their noses using their sweaters or buttoning their flies and tucking in their shirts. It was difficult not to see him do something kind wherever he went. He sometimes walked into the village homesteads to greet people and ate what they ate. He would then listen to traditional stories nodding his head in concentration and laughing at intervals or tell children who flocked around him stories from the Bible. At times he went to the maternal hospital and released mothers who were retained with their new born babies by paying their bills. The people became his people, but I was not sure whether his people would have become their people.

While sitting down the river I saw expectant women who crossed the river and walked four kilometres to reach *Clemência de Deus,* which was a single maternal hospital, too small to serve the large number of women who went there. It was a routine that if the women were crossing the river and were

93

not going to fetch water or work in their farms then they were in a hurry to reach the hospital before they found a long line which would keep them until late in the day. When they came back they faced the wrath of their angry husbands who questioned whether they had shifted roles of making their afternoon meals. Many pregnant women crossed the river during the hot season. My grandfather used to tell me it was because they conceived during the cold seasons when men never left their houses. They woke up early and crossed the river in the icy wind with distended stomachs in groups ranging from newly married to middle ages. They were heard calling their friends, before the cock crowed, to hurry up so that they could book appointments at the hospital.

Far away from civilization, in my home village, a true woman was a baby making machine. The economy and living standards like those in the capital did not allow women to have many children like those in the village where there were vast stretches of land. The point of view was different though because in the village the costs of raising children were defined in terms of food. Clothing and education were not considered as necessities, let alone travel and leisure. The youth there did not go beyond the river where their pieces of land ended but when they did then they were going for special missions like hunting for girls or looking for marriage partners. There was a little girl belonging to Mrs. Fabiano's friend who told me she had been watching movies of families with eight kids. As far as she was concerned it all ended in movies. She asked me endless questions about Africa and even asked me how many kids I would like when I decided to marry.

The girl might not have seen the possibility of such a big family because she had never met with one, but I knew of woman who had twelve children, just across the river. They had only a year between them and their sizes looked like beans that were planted one day apart for twelve days. The husband used to boast of security and wealth around the village and he would be heard shouting at night when drunk that he would set 'dogs' at anyone who dared touch him in the darkness. I did not know how the mother made sure all had eaten but I think it was the most hectic job anyone could have done. There was a day she tore into the silent night with her neighbor whose animals had strayed to her farm and eaten her crops. They shouted at each other from their compounds and let their dirty laundry air out into the neighbourhood. Her neighbor told her that she had so many kids that it was impossible to feed them equally unless she issued them with meal cards.

Polygamy was fading fast in the minds of many people, except in the individuals who had their own reasons and deep in the corners where light was yet to reach like in my home village. My grandfather said the women sired many children to discourage their husbands from bringing home a second wife, something I doubted actually worked for them. The twelve kidded woman's husband had a second wife who was pregnant at the time. Even when it did not work they did not sit to think and talk about it when they met to gossip on their way to the river or when they were plaiting their hairs in their friends' compounds. They spent time thinking more about protecting their marriages than the future of the children. They would be seen malnourished with runny noses playing half naked in the rain which the West described as the true Africa and featured in award winning movies that my baby sister hated to watch.

One day when I was sitting down by the river, I saw an expectant woman who was tired beyond perseverance. It was no surprise that the women in my home village and even beyond went to the mission hospital and delivered the same day then walked several kilometers to their homes to avoid hospital bills, which their husbands would not pay. The woman's hands were at the back of the head and with the way she walked I did not think she would ever reach the hospital. She stopped a couple of times and bent with her hands on the knees and spat before she rose up and tried to walk again. Men never accompanied women to hospitals for maternal reasons, which was a drastic difference from those men in the capital who held hands with their wives and drove them to luxuriant private hospitals. To those in the countryside, child bearing and rearing was a woman's thing. The men were just supervisors and if they found something amiss then the women knew for sure they were in trouble.

The woman almost fell into the river but managed to grab to a tree and sat down. Her time was due and the child was coming in the trees. I closed my book and stood up. There was nobody around who could help when I looked up and down the river. The fact that the process of child birth was purely a woman's affair was my second problem. The closest home had its doors closed and there was no time. I walked down to the woman whose consciousness was fading with labour pains, and I assisted her in giving birth. It was a long time waiting while I supported the head of the baby but it did come out and yell as if it had been practicing how to cry in the womb. It was a fat and handsome baby boy whose eyes were closed in innocence. The woman went away and gave the child both of my names. When my father heard what I had done he insisted I should have called women to do it and warned me against doing the same thing in future. The woman visited our home with the gift of a cock and local vegetables to say her "thanks".

I had assisted one woman and helped save a life. My mind became restless and I asked myself many question why I had done it and what it really meant. I used to think of charity whenever father Agostinho came into my mind, but from that day I became specific in the nature of charity I wanted to do. I dreamt of a hospital which would serve women and children in that place while I was studying and the more time I spent there the more problems I saw them undergo. Speaking as a man I wanted to assist women. Because in that marginalized place they made homes while men made wars. They were not only child-bearing machines but were donkeys as well. They worked in the farm under the scorching sun and then gathered heavy bundles of firewood to go and cater to the needs of the family. They were supposed to make food and warm water for their husbands who went for evening strolls and left them attending to the children. Mrs. Fabiano said one day that she saw a group of men laughing in the streets at a white man who was carrying a baby while his wife was walking freely.

When I started working for a local television network and also wrote articles for the television's leading newspaper, I benefited from an easy access loan for journalists with which I bought seven acres of land that I intended to use to establish the hospital. The land was a strategic two kilometres from my home and six kilometres from the mission hospital. There was another two acres to the east that was for sale at the time, but I was as broke as a desert cockroach. When I talked to the managing director he assisted me in buying the land and told me I could pay him back at my own pace. The people around my home did not know at first why I had bought the piece of land. I did not tell them either, and to my advantage they did not ask. Only a few careless ones told me along the path that I needed to marry if I wanted the land to be used in a proper way. There was my classmate who had dropped out of school to marry and had sired four children in my four years in the school of journalism. When I counted an academic year he counted a child. He told me along the way that education and wealth was nothing without a family. A picture of children with dilapidated looks crossed my mind: runny noses and teary eyes constantly disturbed by flies, standing bare footed in mud, shivering, with torn, dirty vests and wearing nothing from the waist downwards.

Haamid told me about *Gear for a Tear*, which was an Asian charity project funding organisation whose headquarters were in Mumbai. He had worked there for some time and had detailed and valid information about the activities of the organisation. It would take more than a year when a proposal was sent before a response was received, but I was desperate to wait. Their agents then come to inspect the place of the project in question and write reports after which an analysis is made and final results communicated. I wrote a detailed proposal with Haamid's help and submitted it. There was nothing that came on a silver platter, but people still preferred what was on the plate. I remember a management consultant who tried to explain to people in a community project meeting that they needed to work hard for them to achieve something, but I saw that all their minds were elsewhere, planting seeds and fertilizer he had brought them. After his speech they were fighting for the seeds and overpowered security men who left them to struggle. They were people who preferred results over process.

After I secured a good-paying job, there was a man who one day surprised me with his request. I was heading to the house with a newspaper I had bought from the local vendor that carried one of my articles. The man greeted me and when I responded, he told me that he wanted to smoke a cigarette. When I told him I had no problem with it he went ahead and told me that he wanted me to buy him a cigarette. I simply told him that there were things I would not do and kept on walking. He followed me and kept on saying that he was not interested in the large amount of money I earned. He just wanted a few pieces of cigarettes. To send him off I said that I had no money. The previous month was when I had bought the piece of land and the bank had peeled my salary to the bud. It was difficult for a poor person to accept when one said he had no money when he was on the payroll. I stopped and told him casually that I did not tell him to start smoking. It worked and he left me alone.

I was keeping my intentions as secret as possible from the attention of the people and the media. There was the tendency of people killing something that could have helped them before it even started. I had seen projects stumble and dreams killed because people were always afraid of change. Such was the case that happened to a Congolese preacher who set up a talent school and would nurture talent in street children then connect them to sports and other opportunities. He was gunned down in cold blood and his academy set ablaze by unknown people. It was barely a week after an Italian priest got himself into trouble by saying that he was staying in a bandit country when explaining why he had so many lawyers and bodyguards. Religious leaders and politicians called for his deportation over the utterances. Some people seized the opportunity to enrich themselves deep from wells of selfishness and gluttonous intentions within them.

It was seen in places like along Thika Road. Money was just money and so it was made through any means. When means of making cash became scarce, even churches became businesses and they sprung up day and night like grass in the Savannah at the fall of rain. They conveyed the message of giving and believers became their customers; therefore, whenever their numbers became considerable they reaped more by calling for foreign donations. Disagreements emerged when their accounts were stashed with money and differences in expenditures arose. The leaders split as a result to start their own churches. When the numbers did not multiply as they wanted, they staged crusades and shows in markets and roadsides to reap fame advantage, and it worked like magic because their numbers swelled within days. The economy was bad and times were changing from the ages of religious respect and trust to the times of conmen and blackmail. Mrs. Fabiano said she had sat in a church where she saw a believer, sitting near a priest, check his phone several times to make sure it was there.

I told Meyer one day that he had enjoyed donkey delicacy when a person reported to a local police station that his four donkeys were missing, but he could not believe it. When we did a media investigation we found out that the donkeys were slaughtered kilometres away and ended up in a butchery where he had bought meat and enjoyed it that evening thinking it was beef. The skins, legs and heads were dumped in the bush nearby, providing undeniable evidence of what had happened. When I told him the real story three days after he walked to the sink and vomited as if there was a blade of grass in his throat. We had argued sometime back about the suitability of donkey meat for human consumption after which he insisted the animal looked poisonous. Nothing was left to chance when it came to making money. An animal could not stray a few metres day or night without being converted into something more valuable.

Anyone who wanted an overnight rise from rags to riches needed to accept that money was just money. It did not apply though to people like me who were trying to rise from a low level to something more comfortable. Everybody wants to rise from poverty to richness, but nobody wants to fall from richness to poverty. Because of the either way realities involved, people tend to panic when thinking about moving from one state to the other. It is not a surprise because people are always afraid of change regardless of status. Maybe, it is the panic and the status of poverty which make poor people to see richness as something bad. My sister used to wonder why families with enough food had a difficult time telling children to eat, while in poor families' children did not need to be told to eat because they hovered around the food long before it was cooked. They would peep from windows and doors whenever visitors were eating or wait in the kitchen to scavenge on leftovers. They would be heard crying at the back of their houses when their mothers pinched their cheeks to send them away from dining tables. In rich families kids would be heard threatening the help that they would not eat, which sent kids from poor families in the neighbourhood salivating like the young ones of a homecoming eagle.

Much as the structure of bad parenting contributed to family related problems, it did not occur to me before that children could send a great family crawling on the ground until I saw with my own eyes what happened to one rich family who had settled in the countryside to invest. We might not have been a rich family, but at the same time we were not a struggling family, I understood what poverty meant by looking at the way other people lived in the neighbourhood. At least we did not sleep hungry and we could afford shelter over our heads and something to cover our bodies. When I was growing up, it was not easy for a vehicle to pass along the rough road which stretched to the south. Children in rags rushed to the roads to have a look at the human driven machine which was rare in the village. The only vehicle around was that of Father Agostinho and those which were stationed at the *Clemência de Deus*. Even elderly people peeped from their farms or watched from the roadsides where they sat to pass time by basking their soap smeared bodies in the sun.

The rich family settled in the village and built a large scale timber store whose customers came from various towns. There were cheap raw materials from the cheap large number of trees people owned on their farms. With time they opened two retail shops and the only grain mill within six kilometres. They used to come to the Sunday school with a saloon car and their offering was in terms of cheques. The family comprised of two beautiful daughters and a small boy whose father was a former sales marketer in Canada. He came back to the country after he had spent twenty years abroad. The mother of the family had worked as an agricultural field extension officer in the country for several years. It was a feared family because of its great history, so the people had a strong feeling that the only thing between themselves and the family was the village and the trees they sold to their store. They got out of the way when their children passed to avoid contact because they knew if something happened to the children, they did not stand a chance.

As time went by and the girls grew to teenagers, the family started growing. Not because the parents decided to extend it but the girls sired children while still in their parent's home. The elder one had four children by the time she was in mid-secondary level while the second one had two. As it became in most cases the prospects of education started narrowing and like many before them, they turned to drugs and alcohol. They would disappear from home or sneak away from school to wander in houses of entertainment as much they as wanted, spending huge sums of stolen money from their investments. Their brother followed suit soon afterwards. They rotated around towns and cells then finally dropped out of school. One day they were involved in a drug trafficking circus along the strip of the coast and were nabbed by the authorities. The family used all its resources in the case but by the time they were set free the only thing in their possession was water and soil like everyone else.

To cater for their children, the girls walked from one farm to the other looking for casual jobs and if they were lucky they were allocated pieces of land to dig and lines of tea to pick. The mother, who helplessly watched her family perish, went into a coma soon after suffering a major stroke. She died shortly after her son was given a life sentence for committing a violent robbery. It is said that children are a blessing, but I then knew well that some children were a curse. They had dropped from richness to poverty rather than rise from poverty to richness. The people who thought they were failures in their lives found voice to discuss about what had happened, telling each other how money and richness was bad. They stood a distance away looking at the girls working on farms with blunt hoes with rough handles which formed calluses on their soft hands.

The people who used to step aside for them to pass laughed and cheered that at long last they were on the same level, which they considered reality. Men slept with the girls in turns, considering it a lifetime achievement for a family which was once untouchable, and women gave them clothes to wash down by the river for few coins. They would then gather around them down in the local market where they were hired to sell vegetables and fruits giving them tips on how one needed to survive bad prices. They then demanded to hear what had happened continuously, not to help them, but to get the first-hand versions meant for gossiping with their age mates during their free time. Men used to tell the father of the home that a drink helped to pass the day unnoticed. He later developed insanity and went to live in the dirty corners of the horticulture market.

Chapter Six

The Portuguese family was gathering at the Nairobi arboretum to celebrate its culture and diversity for one week. Excitation and anxiety greeted the preparations a couple of days before the material day. There were signs that it was going to be great. At least Mrs. Fabiano assured us that it was going to be good. We had learnt to trust her word, and whenever she spoke nobody doubted her. We received a letter of invitation from the Portuguese embassy which recognised and appreciated Mark's as one of the few Portuguese institutions and therefore our presence at the function would have been of great importance. I was also longing for the day to meet people from different parts of the world to see what they did and how they spoke. There were a lot of invited guests picked from various African countries and different parts of the world. It was a rare opportunity for people like us to see if we had learnt enough about the language and to consider more the prospects of what we were doing. The classes of the week were rescheduled and those before were hurried.

On the same day we received an invitation letter from the embassy, sad news came from the mission hospital back at home that Father Alberto Agostinho had passed away. It had been a long time since he went back to his country but his service and dedication was fresh in the eyes and minds of the people he had crossed borders to help for free. He was the ambassador of life back in the village when he initiated building the mission hospital without which the women back there would never have seen the joy of having children. I remembered his award which I kept in record as one of my achievements. On the tearful farewell ceremony he pinched Russel's cheeks and patted my back because I had dedicated my time and money taking care of Russel. The people had rubbished it saying I had chosen to take care of the child to enable me solicit foreign aid and attract Western sympathy. Even though they said so, they were all united in sadness that Father Agostinho was going away with no probability of coming back. To me he was unique; he even touched the hearts of the people there who were harder to please than melting a stone using a tin lamp.

It was sad to remember that his kindness, as odd as he looked in the village, was the one thing which kept me going to the Sunday school like many others. He was the one who inspired me to learn his language and I hoped that perhaps one day I would tell him so when we met. I wanted to show him how far I had come. Unfortunately, that was not going to be possible because he was not able to keep the distance between life and death. It was painful to remember how good he was when he used to wipe the runny noses of children in Sunday school, and help them button up their flies. There were no signs of anyone like him who could have existed in that place any time in the future. I still heard his voice in my mind when he used to say there was a time for living and a time for dying as he officiated masses in funerals. Even when he went away he kept on sending a helping hand to the women and children back at the hospital who could not pay even the subsidised hospital bills. Now that he was dead it was going to be even more difficult.

Among the most important activities which were to be carried out during the week was that, for the first time a Portuguese club was going to be formed in the country. During the seven day event elections were to be carried out for the prestigious positions of the club. The businessmen were expected to take advantage of the week to advertise Portuguese products and exploit various economic opportunities. There would be numerous Portuguese restaurant representatives who would be there to show what they had. Much as I knew about Portuguese dishes I had never tasted any and it was going to be fun to see and taste what they offered in those restaurants. In one of the mentoring programmes, the hall broke into laughter when professor Nairit said that the dishes which had the fewest spices in the world were African dishes. That made me remember a Greek tourist who said that he had been warned that when someone is in Africa he should be careful about what he eats, especially meat. Meat might have been just meat because in some places chimpanzees and even human flesh was a delicacy. It might have been true or false but I think professor Nairit was a little racial. There was no single day he attached a value to us. He was always a constant complainer.

Visitors and invited guests arrived and camped in luxurious hotels in the capital awaiting the material day. To us, who spent hours up and down lecture halls, it was a break from things involving commitment as students welcomed the suspension of lessons until the function was over. Breaking the monotony was vital but I could see it came with different intentions. There were those who wanted to take time off and disappear until the function was over as well as those who were excited about the event they were attending for the first time in their lives, while few more wanted to meet new people and see how they behaved. Others like me wanted to meet new ideas in the rare important step of making the world smaller as all of us were keen on the new culture and decide with time whether it was something worth going on record. There were many organised language functions such as that one, but only interested groups were keen on it in a multilingual incubator such as Mark's.

The Portuguese ambassador Diogo Carlito was a great friend of Mrs. Fabiano. He called her and insisted our presence at the function was going to be highly appreciated. She called me that evening and gave me a hectic job of preparing a Portuguese speech. I had hoped she would pick someone else but I could not refuse because I knew she had seen value in me. I understood what it meant when a mother continuously picks one child for an errand in a family of many children. I had no doubt that I spoke Portuguese better than I could write it, which was the opposite case with Tracy, who garnered good grades in writing every time there was an examination. When it came to speaking it one would have thought she was chewing bones. I called her and sought her help in writing as I kept on laughing about the way she pronounced some of the words. I would easily tell that her mind was away as she kept on shifting attention from what we were doing to something which kept her uncomfortable and sad.

After I had gone through my speech I went to the balcony to enjoy the evening breeze. The coldness of the past few days was engulfed by warm currents which flew around soothing and reassuring the hearts of the people who clung to life. It was calm outside there and the people were onto their usual evening activities. They were happy and shouting from left to right and lighting their faces with smiles up and down the streets. Death had suspended hunting them down when it was frustrated by yielding efforts which supported life. They kept the distance and there was no sign that it was going to be narrowed soon. That was why even the giant owl was silent that night and it kept its hooting to itself. It was dark up the tree with covered skies but I knew it was somewhere up there on the tree. It was the end of the month and people were back in their good moods again. Their bank accounts had driven away loneliness and credit cards were full. Wives reconciled with their husbands and promised each other to work together, insisting they needed to forget about their past differences.

The historical road was ever busy. That was the only thing which never changed. It was a complicated road that was highly valued for several economic and academic reasons. It carried a whole load of learning institutions, all the way from the capital to where it knotted its end in the industrial area kilometres away. Many people who were basking on academic glory and nice jobs had first set their foot on that road. It did not only destroy lives but made them as well. That was what many people did not understand. It depended on how one interpreted it. The first thing to come to anyone's mind whenever the name of the road was mentioned were the traffic jams. Then multi-practices followed, which were as a result of the notoriety crafted in the minds of people who were trying to earn a living. When I first set my foot on that road I was cautious like everyone else but time killed caution and that was what I was afraid of losing. The first time people came here they hated it but with time they would talk about how much they hated it without ever thinking of going away.

I had hoped that Haamid would be there on the opening day but he had some other commitments. I was not a person to expect much from social functions, and I needed someone who would keep us talking. Haamid was good at making friends and that was because he did not forget himself for too long. I knew that it would get lonely somewhere because I spent more time studying people than making friends with them. I understood what happened in such functions and did not see why that one would have been different. The first thing would have been meeting and then knowing each other after which familiarising followed. That was the point where people started splitting into groups and pairing up. Anyone who remained alone was barred by social boundaries and it would not take long before such a scenario happened. I was feeling like a victim of loneliness before the function even started and that was my biggest worry. Tracy was good but it was not her company I wanted that day. I wanted someone who would cheer other people up, even falsely, so long as they became happy.

It was going to be interesting to see what people from different parts of the world thought about each other. The previous week in Professor Nairit's programme, an Italian youth who represented his father in a charity mission in the country talked to us as if we were stupid children. What he forgot, and the students did not mind telling him, was that in Africa, there was no such thing as playing it cool when things were not going well. I did not know who had coached him that when one was in such a place he needed to teach people about common sense. At one time he asked the treasurer whether he knew how to store a number in a cell phone when he asked for his contacts and on the other he nodded in encouragement when someone brought him ice cream in the sun like he was training a monkey on implications of weather. Despite the fact that he was from Rome, he didn't understand the expression "When in Rome, do as the Romans do." While he was in Africa, I did not know if he knew how to act. Those who had sent him to represent his father did not tell him that he needed to behave like a wizard in order to help a wizard. Trouble began when he warned someone against whispering when he was speaking. The students called him names and stormed out of the meeting.

Among the visitors was Mrs. Fabiano's daughter, Adelina Christina, who was studying Economics at the University of Lisboa. She had jetted from Lisboa two days before. Her mother joked that she always wanted to come and see Africa, but she had refused because she was afraid she would go back with all the African men who would have done anything to get her. She said that for all the years she had travelled around the world there was nothing stubborn than an African man with his eye on the prize. It looked like at long last she had accepted she needed to be present at that important function. They say that "seeing is believing" and it was a question of time for her to decide whether she liked Africa. She was fascinated by the animals deep in the Masaai Mara where she had spent the day before. No one in history ever went there and came out thinking it was boring.

Her mother trusted her with me. She had to attend to an emergency in town and would miss the first day of the event. I was sure that Mrs. Fabiano was aware that I did not know how to entertain a visitor, even though she knew that it was not difficult for me to initiate a conversation. One thing I quickly noticed was that Adelina was not a girl with big expectations. She used her eyes more that her mouth, and in order to know how she felt one needed to look at her eyes because she made observations without a facial expression. She had arrived with her mother's heavy Range Rover and I could see similarities between mother and daughter.   Mrs. Fabiano liked driving heavy vehicles which were thought to be owned by men. I knew that she had information about that but she was a woman who lived her life to the fullest. She needed no consultations when deciding what was best for her and those who were waiting were wasting their time. Adelina was the same only that she was kinder. She did not ask many questions and did not expect them either. She was wearing a light blue pullover in that misty morning and a white dress with big red flowers. Her kindness had something to do with her simplicity, and I felt that as we entered the famous arboretum.

There were several reasons why Mrs. Fabiano bestowed her trust on me whenever she wanted someone reliable. First, she was a strict woman and did not allow the harmlessness she portrayed to other people materialise into weakness. She easily changed moods depending on the situation. There were times when she laughed and times when she meant business. If anyone took time with her, he or she would have realised that the strictness looked like an adjustment she made along the way. She had an inward hatred for people who spent too much time talking and doing things for fun. She loved hardworking people, especially those who meant business. I saw it in her on the day she knew that apart from being young and a student, I was already earning good salary as an investigative journalist. She looked at me, raised her eyebrows then nodded her head. Having seen such values, it did not matter to her whether someone was always at smiles or not. She recognised hard work and dedication. I realised that it was what she wanted to build for her daughter who, like me, spent much of the time in her own world.

The Nairobi arboretum was alive with activities and people were streaming in every minute. We received nice a welcome and precise directions on where we were supposed to be and what we needed to do. Adelina's mother was right when she said that the event was going to be good. Portuguese greetings hit the air in their raw accent and soon the English I was used to had become a sterile function. Even when we lied to each other that we were sheltering under one umbrella that day, there were silent differences which bit deep into the confidence of many in that social gathering. Some people were pleased to make friends and mingle while more others were cautious about which groups to make friends with. There was a wave dictating sense of direction but with time I saw that it was disappearing with more open conversations and interactions. That was what took us there, but I did not know it would take time to turn around.

It occurred to me that I was the only friend Adelina knew and she needed my company at least for that time. I did not know how long she was going to stay silent like that and if at all she was planning to make friends. She just looked like one of my versions but she was not a writer so I failed to understand her silence. I attended a religious function which meant to unite Christian organisations in East Africa and towards the end the chief priest told us to pair up and gave us a full hour to interact. The girl I had paired up with expected me to start a conversation like all girls did, but I had no information on what type of conversation she wanted. I started talking about life and career and the importance of religion in society. At first she nodded and listened carefully but with time became disinterested and her mind went elsewhere. She moved away and went to pair up with someone else. That was when I realised how boring I was when it came to cheering someone up. She had expected me to tell her that it was nice to meet her and that if she did not mind, that we could go date in the neighbouring luxuriant Nairobi.

There were men in and out of tents who stood with cups of coffee telling the ladies they found that it was nice meeting them and hoped to get familiar fast so that they could ask them out on a date later after the function. They said it all in the smiles on their faces and unhurried talks which indicated that they were careful to choose their words so that they would stand a chance. That was how people interpreted social functions and it was what kept them around. What the ladies knew and the men did not know was that those chats were short interviews like any first date of a relationship. There were others, like me or Adelina, who were less interested in such kind of social arts. Maybe that was why we stood watching what was going on silently. I served two cups of coffee and brought Adelina one. We moved away from the hugging people and new arrivals to the giant species of trees which had difficult scientific names on pieces of wood nailed on them. She told me stories about Lisbon and I told her about what happened in Nairobi and everything she needed to know about what she did not see. She would talk but only if she was given time and she knew a great deal of what the world was and what it did.

After I delivered a fine Portuguese speech that morning, head ambassador Diogo Carlito wanted to see me when the speaker said that I represented Mrs.

Fabiano. The visitors kept on applauding throughout the speech, impressed by quite fine Portuguese in a country which was not dominated by the language. I did not do it to look good but whenever I was given a commitment I took time to do my part. I highlighted the importance of various nationalities and the need for stronger ties. I appreciated the presence of the visitors and thanked our institution for providing us with the opportunity to learn languages and cultures of other people. I challenged the Portuguese and Brazilian embassies to arrange and coordinate more exchange programmes insisting on the need for the youth to unite. I told the visitors to feel welcome and enjoy themselves, careful not to caution anyone against anything. In such a function and with such type of people it was not about telling them what it was supposed to be but what they wanted to hear.

While the visitors applauded every single effort that day, many locals were full of criticism whenever a single mistake was found I overhead a person telling another that even when most people agreed I had given a nice speech, whites were like children and clapped at anything. They were the same people who isolated themselves and stood in groups watching the fun of the event from a distance. When they were tired of talking about what they did not like, they conspired on how to prey on college girls who graced the event. They would be seen throwing their eyes in all directions like squirrels in a maize store. They did not take away heavy bunches of keys from their hands nor did they stray far away from vehicles of their bosses because they would be required any time. When they stood talking to ladies they motioned towards the vehicles they drove and touched the collars of their shirts. The ladies gave them pending confirmations and strolled around to see if they would find someone better. When they did not, they accepted to go out with them. It was an endless game that benefitted the highest bidders.

The Brazilian and Portuguese embassies looked more united even when they were separated by borders of continents. After the speeches were over that morning we were entertained by good music from the two countries. There was an impressive performance of *Rumba Portuguesa* from top musicians in Portugal. I did not know there was such good music and great talent hiding in Europe. The people entered the empty space to dance to the music as glasses clinked in cheers up in the air. Adelina took my hand and we joined them dancing. She was a good dancer and dancing together helped us neutralise our differences. For the first time I saw her smile revealing beautiful white teeth. She was a flower which hid its petals away from insects of pollination, but above all she was happy. The conclusion I had developed in my mind was that she would find me boring and leave me. We belonged to one in spite of our differences in colour or the lives we led.

I was having a great break from the usual introductions I was used to. Among my natives, what followed after names and place were stories about the weather and how crops were doing, or the differences in their market prices. Among the visitors, what followed names and place was what someone was doing, and I could not help feeling professional when I said I was a journalist. It was a long time since someone asked me what I was doing and a weird sense of belonging lit my heart. In the village and in the streets it was an offensive question to ask people what they were doing. They would quote numerous activities depending on how the day broke, but it all meant that they were doing nothing. I learnt the difference between what someone was doing and what exactly he was doing when one day a visiting British doctor told a boy working as a sales promoter that he was aware that he did sales promotion but he wanted to know what he did exactly. According to the doctor, some careers were branches and others were leaves but one needed to have trunk-and -root careers as basics.

When Brazilians took to the stage to perform *samba de gafieira,* which was a type of Brazilian dance called samba, we went to sit behind the tent. The morning sunlight promised that it would not rain at least for that day. The giant trees stood in dark green, defiant against the pollution of the great capital city. They grew day and night without stop because they had maximum protection from conservationists. There were a number of climbing plants coiling around then to the top so that they would catch a glimpse of the free sunlight every morning. The arboretum was the place to be when one wanted to think away from the storeys and roads. It was a place for people like me because it reminded me of the great peaceful times I used to have down by the river when I was still young. Adelina was an average English speaker but we opted to talk in Portuguese. I had never talked to someone in Portuguese before except when communicating with Mrs. Fabiano.

"There are several divisions of that kind of dance in my country," she said.

"I love the beats of the song of this one. Which one is your favourite type among the divisions?" I asked.

"Oh…any one of them. I'm not that specific. It depends on how it is played or performed because they are artists who really know how to play them."

Even when she said that I felt that she did not listen nor was she interested about the songs much.

She took out juice bottles from her bag and handed me one. She then took out some biscuits and used her lap as the table.

"My mother likes you," she said.

"I like her too. Well, we all do," I said.

She sipped her juice then looked at a group of people who were going into the trees and taking photographs.

"She wants you to be friends," she said.

"How is that a possibility?" I wondered.

She laughed mockingly.

"I do not know either," she said.

"It is not easy to tell what my mother likes about someone."

I knew she did not understand. What I meant was that I was always alone in the things I did and the only way I managed to move forward was to think quickly. I was always apologetic that I did not wait for opinions except in dilemma standoffs, and I always got through it using my own means. That was the way I grew up and changing it in adulthood would have made me confused.

Whenever someone was in something, he did not realise its value until he was out of it. Born in South America and brought up in Europe, those parts of the world everyone thought were containers of money and high standards of living did not fascinate her anymore. While natives spent nights thinking about how they would get away from Africa to see the world, others were dying to go there. I saw it with many couples who came from far and wide to settle and do farming in the areas of our country which experienced long periods of drought. They left the cities of gold and towns of merry to come and confine themselves to semi-arid areas where winds blew up the loose soil that had little or no cover. They stayed in the places where there were no night clubs or family reunions. If there was a word to go with it then I think that was what was called the magic of Africa. Some people preferred staying in the wild because they had been brought up in cities and those who were brought up in the wild spent nights thinking about cities.

In one of her visits, when Father Alberto's niece visited and we attended the sermon in the same church, she accompanied her uncle for the afternoon tour of people in the village. Given the humbleness of such an activity he left her on her own to talk and make friends with fellow teenagers in the village. I remember her getting excited when she blew fire with her mouth until it burst into flames in the three-stoned fireplace typical of the traditional African kitchen of one of our neighbours. To her it looked like fun to make food using such a setup. She walked with a large group of excited half-naked children following behind her. They were natives who always wondered what part of the world such people came from. I overheard one day children arguing that if one stopped working at the farm and drank milk and honey, his skin would be like that of a white man. One of them disagreed and said that when they were recovering from a circumcision in the house for three weeks their skins turned brown and that one needed to confine himself for a number of days.

The adventurous tour turned ugly later in the day when a boy got himself into trouble by thinking she was one of those village maidens they raped when they went to the river. He was a school dropout as early as elementary who joined the rest of the people who formed a heavy load for the country's budgeting. Like all people running away from everything and seeking refuge in something, he had found the usual available things to lean on, obviously local liquor and stealing tobacco from old men's gardens then competing with friends of the same level on who could drink more without getting drunk and take the longest puff from tobacco sticks they modified from old newspapers. He had gained himself praise by digging large farms for a few shillings which added him nothing other than walking on the pride that he provided the heaviest labour force for the lowest price. With time his handsome teenage body faded to an old tree struck by lightning. People cheered him when he was drunk but what was interesting was that he never stopped to ask himself why. Like many others before him and those who were to follow, he would not account for his behaviour.

As a cover up of his ill lifestyle he called himself the bad boy who never harvested honey using a fire. It was a saying back in the village when talking about "real men." The people simply called him "the bad boy" until it overtook his real name. They would be heard shouting at him along village paths in the morning "bad boy! bad boy!" Then he responded by saying, "Who does not harvest honey using a fire!" With time he forgot and thought he was a real bad boy and would harvest honey from any hive without using a fire but he did not know that some bee hives were hostile to that approach. He thought father Agostinho's niece was harmless and therefore as easy as stealing tobacco from the farm. He approached her, but she refused him. He thought she had refused because his skin was black and so he told her that in the past he was Indian before he became a black native. When she started laughing he took it as a yes and started dragging her to a nearby hut the way he did to village maidens. The attempted rape earned him sixteen years in a maximum security prison.

Even when I had arrived in Mrs. Fabiano's luxuriant Range Rover I knew there were a lot of differences between people in that function. The minister of tourism had challenged locals by telling them to get married to foreigners when he was reading the country's tourism statistics of the year. He boasted that he had married a German while he was doing his masters abroad. I was looking at the locals in that function and realised their nervousness was not on their faces but surely it was in their hearts. They had arrived by school buses while the foreigners drove expensive private vehicles. I did not even know whether there was a single man there who would pay the expenses of a date in town if he was ever given one. The events which followed after the locals arranged their own dates were laughable. The men kept on checking their wallets in toilets to make sure they had enough cash for cooling down bills before the next salary.

There was something behind Adelina's simplicity which was difficult to understand. When she was talking to her fellow citizens, she shook their hands and nodded her head then smiled briefly after which she looked away to some memory I would tell she did not like. There was a precaution she was taking when she talked to the visitors because she was brief with introductions and did not encourage and extensive talk. It then occurred to me that she did not want to be alone, but she wanted to feel lonely. She was a strange kind of a girl. It was not easy to know what went on in people's minds and Adelina had a secretive mind even more difficult to read because one would not have obtained even a single clue by talking to her. She was a good listener and nodded her head when I was talking to her, after which she gave brief comments without giving any related example or what she thought about what we were talking about. Then as she leaned on a tree with crossed arms listening to a boy who was talking to her she kept on pulling her hair to the back and nodding her head without reacting to it verbally.

Ambassador Carlito was surprised to learn that I was a journalist when we held a private talk late in the evening. He had worked in Australia years before in a private firm where Maria Fabiano was his secretary back then, and coincidence had sent them working together again in the same country years after. He talked to me like I was familiar to him and I could see that he was more interested in my Portuguese and the future plans I had after college. He said that he had come to East Africa to stay and had no intentions of leaving after he had spent several years in various parts of the world in his country's service. He had travelled near and far, heard and saw things which made him feel he needed rest somewhere along the stretch where he would call destiny away from endless human activities of making and spending money. There were activities of establishing and modifying which entailed building and destroying to best suit circumstances. Having stayed eight years in the country he had come to like East Africa and its people. He had witnessed the birth of the East African Community and looked forward to its success.

Carlito's two children, Celestino and Elisa, were in South Africa studying mass communication and Vetinary Medicine respectively. He told me he had no intentions of influencing their choices on where they wanted to be in their life. Their mother was then the executive director in a beef production firm in Brazil, the country which was the world's chief beef producer at the time. Occupational reasons kept them away from each other for a long time, and they only managed to stay in touch by the privileges of modern communication and technology. As a matter of fact Ambassador Carlito, who was then in his late sixties, was looking for potential people and friends who would serve as terms of reference in his plan to invest and establish quickly before his term in office expired in two years' time. Much as he wanted his children to stay where they thought best in the world he wished that his family would accept to stay with him once his plans materialised.

After I parted with Ambassador Carlito and promised to stay in touch, I joined the others in having lunch and making friends before the day started frowning away. Preparations for the party, which was expected to start from the early hours of the evening until the next morning, were underway. Those children of darkness had started moving closer and having more straight talks because they knew their time was nearing. All of a sudden the differences between the people disappeared. They seemed to be pulling together and accepting that all of them were human. As the first and successful day of the function started fading, they sat in groups without the colours of their skins or the accent of their languages on their minds. They talked and joked or danced to the music. Once again they represented a world which anyone would have longed for. They said the language of love penetrated well in darkness when the lights turned low, and those who loved each other knew their time was approaching.

The sun disappeared without notice, leaving behind an orange illumination on the horizon where it had sunk. Those who wanted to be happy in the arboretum were different from the people in the capital who changed their plans each and every minute to survive. It was not all of them who survived but each and every one of them were optimistic that they would. The secret to survival was that one needed to pull out a strategy and believe in it, even if it was a bright guesswork full of fallacy. The people lied to the capital but the capital told them the truth. The night reminded them that it was time to sleep even when they went about doing different activities in the darkness. The which day they so much hated to see, reminded them that they needed to work and fend for themselves and their families, which they regretted having. The warm evening breeze did not stop to soothe them and their activities. They would do anything they wanted from hating to loving it but the capital was always there laughing at them.

After the party had begun, Adelina left a group she was chatting with and came to where I was standing at the hedge of the trees looking towards the direction where the sun had disappeared. The coldness brought by the trees had begun to bite but the blowing wind prevented it from becoming unbearable, by constantly mixing it with the day's heat gathered from roads of the city and vehicles which had spent the day transporting people and goods. We sat on the dry leaves facing the direction away from Thika Road. The sky above the horizon where the sun had sunk was still orange as if taking itself out of blame for the darkness by indicating where the vital source of light had gone missing. She opened her heart and told me about the history of her family. Her only brother, Fernando, who had since died from gun shots in the streets of Mexico, seemed to have changed their lives forever. He had dropped out of high school after her parent's divorce and went to live with his father who was working as a chemical engineer then in the United States. She paused in between words when she told me how her brother was caught in the crossfire in a drug related shooting. She was a strong girl who compressed tears to smiles of pain and her politeness absorbed the shock of her disintegrated family that was not likely to reunite.

My eyes met with those of Irene when I looked towards the second tent. She smiled and winked. When Adelina saw it, she licked her lips and turned her eyes into the darkness of the trees. It was difficult to know how Irene managed to penetrate the tight security which was beefed up, especially when darkness fell. I was not surprised after I read her diaries. She was a girl who penetrated walls and gates, crashed executives' parties then left any time she wanted without anyone even knowing she was there. The effects she left behind were realised when she was gone, but she erased tracks so that finding her was an exercise in futility. As she danced slowly to the sound of music and as beautiful as she looked to the red and orange lights, nobody would have denied that she represented something special which had no logical theory and that was why those rich foreigners did not know that they were playing with fire. They were pleased by her generosity and they danced with her in turns telling her she was a good dancer because she had a huge experience for such.

The clock ticked by and the people did not like the rate at which time elapsed. The lights of some buildings in the capital went off one-by-one. Those which remained on were dimmed and their colours altered. The party went on and the people formed

125

circles to dance and have fun. Those who were tired of the party went to different places of entertainment around the capital. Ladies changed into different dresses to suit the darkness and went to attend dates they had promised during the day. The area in close proximity to the arboretum was dark, apart from a faint light from street lights in the distance. Everything looked strange in the darkness and it seemed that secrets of the capital came out during the night never to be known because they disappeared during the day. Even Adelina was silent in the half-light, but I could tell she was sad. A fire fly flickered somewhere in the trees lighting up was as it flew through the branches of the great canopies.

Chapter Seven

My roommate, Meyer, behaved like a person who made a deal with God to live forever. His lifestyle was kept alive by numerous concubines who seemed to agree that coincidence was a common word in infidelity. He was a plumber of his own game that had a series of interconnected illicit affairs. An expert, he must have been, because rarely was there a leak in his connections where love making flowed smooth and defined like oil from a refining plant. What happened between himself and his concubine at a single time existed, while in the minds of those who came in thereafter, it never existed. He had done an irreparable damage to his sense of pride, and to kill ill intentions that had established in his mind, was as impossible as trying to hit the moon with a stone. What I knew while in the field collecting information for my job was that what happened somewhere happened everywhere. The players were different but the game was the same. It was an easy thing to see it in another person but more difficult to see it in oneself and that was why Irene always criticized Meyer. Insane people never agreed on the way they looked at things. They saw each other as being in separate categories of insanity and might have agreed on some issue, however crazy it looked, but as a psychiatrist would have said, it was not because they would have agreed on everything; it was because they were insane.

An old man sat on the balcony of the fourth floor of a building across the road pulling on his old accordion, lively as if he was playing a lullaby to the people who lived in that late hour of the night. It was a time people said they had slept and "came up" for the second consecutive time. It was a phrase that the people commonly used to describe waking up at intervals during the night. The security light illuminated the white hair of his unmoving head, which made him look like a photograph in a music history book. He wore a white vest in the cold and did not look like he cared for the health of his tired body. His concentration was on his instrument, so much that he was not even aware of the mosquitoes and night insects that flew around him. He had a wealth of knowledge about natural phenomena and I did not think he needed someone to tell him that he needed an overcoat to cover his dry hands. He pulled one soft rhythm after another and the people liked it even in their sleep. That was why Meyer cleared his throat and started snoring louder. The man looked older than the road itself and looked satisfied with the life he had lived because different things interested him. He had slept enough in his life and that was why he was playing his instrument long into the night.

There were times when a man became interested in things other than his life and that of the family. The accordion was the dearest thing to the man on the balcony, while Meyer felt he had not enjoyed his life to the fullest. There was a runaway man with a sack of maize flour strapped at the back of his bicycle in the village who got tired with his family after he realised that they were just a bunch of consumers who always waited to feed on his sweat. He claimed that when he married he thought life was going to be good but as time went by and they had children, he realised he should have waited a little longer. Because it was his family, he decided to regulate consumption of flour as a basic in his kitchen. He measured an amount of flour for cooking and then scribbled a signature with his finger to make sure it was not touched while he was away. When they discovered the signature he changed to foot prints of a hen. He would make a hen step on the flour and then he took note of the pattern. When they discovered that, he started strapping the remaining flour at the back of his bicycle and he would take it wherever he went.

The wife of the man would put a pot of water on the fire, and when it was almost at its boiling point, she would walk out to the road to see if she could see his bicycle. Whenever someone was walking to the direction he left after the last meal she sent a message for him to be told that the water was boiling and children were hungry. If the message reached him he would be seen speeding down the slope with his bicycle, his shirt flapping against the wind. He delivered the meal's measurement and then went away until the meal was ready. Children gathered by the roadside shouting at him "runaway man with a weighing machine in his eyes!" until he disappeared at the bend. The runaway man did not get annoyed with them. Sometimes he distributed them guavas he picked from the trees of the farms he worked. Sometimes rain fell when he was coming home from work and he always told his wife and children that it was their consumption and dishonesty which made the flour wet.

Meyer was worse than the runaway man because his art of love was pure selfishness. That was what I learnt the more I found out about Eve, the girl who claimed to be his girlfriend. Sometimes she cooked for him and spent the night there, then woke up in the morning to catch the bus to school. She was one of the teenagers whose life was governed by a strong emotion called love. Like the days of the merry making students of Mark's, she did not have a time and season for everything. She was loyal and dedicated but that alone failed to give her a guarantee of getting them in return. In other words, she was lying to herself about her love for him, and she knew this because sometimes she tried to change him but she refused to accept it. That was why she was there for a number of days. She was taking care of something that had long taken care of itself. The confidence of her decision to hang around there whenever she felt like was strengthened by members of her family who let everyone do what pleased them. I heard her many times telling Meyer that she had been told to finish household chores before she came over.

In many families, firstborns always suffered the consequence of experiment before the parents learnt practical details of children's stages and progressed more naturally in those who followed. Those who came first carried all the crosses of trial and error purely on their own for the sake of those who came after them. When parents were away from home they took full responsibility of making sure nothing went wrong and had authority over the behaviour of younger siblings. Most people believed that if the firstborns went off track the rest of the siblings followed but, if they became successful, the rest of the siblings were likely to succeed as well because they were crucial role models of the family. Being the first child in our family I did not feel the heat of expectations except on very limited occasions. I grew up on my own and decided what was good for me because my father rarely commented on what he thought about me. He just expected me to take masculine responsibility, rather than just being the first child of the family. At my home, stepmothers had no voice over what was expected of the children that were already present in the home; therefore, there was respect of distance between me and my stepmother.

The things I did or the decisions I made were not because I was expected to. In our community, the eldest son was supposed to substitute his father when he was away from family property. A decision by the eldest son was taken the same as that of the father. My father was different and did not expect me to act on his behalf. I grew up knowing that, to him, I would be a child forever like my sister Tracy. He never consulted me, even in important family matters. What he did not tell me, but I'm sure he wanted me to know, was that he expected me to behave like a man. There was an incident when a neighbour cut down one of our trees and used it for fencing. I was barely eight then. The tree was lying on the border, making it difficult to tell who the owner was, which caused some confusion. The tree had grown without interference but remained disputed for a long time. When my father came back he asked me what I did after the neighbour cut down the tree. When I did not give him the answer he wanted he went ahead and called me a woman in long trousers. He was the kind of father who expected me to behave like a man but did not treat me like one.

Because I grew up knowing I had no authority over anyone, all the rules I made were mine, and I did not expect them to touch anyone else. That was why some people thought I was selfish when it came to making decisions. When I was telling my baby sister how she was supposed to handle herself I did it like some form of advice rather than just dos and don'ts. I then grew up without confidence of leadership, considering myself as unripe to make a lead that anyone would follow. Even when my sister understood many things and told me that I was her role model, the guilt of defeat failed to leave me. That was why I saw it as a difficult thing to tell Eve that she was wrong on the path she had chosen as a young girl. She seemed to have sensed that I was not up to making friends and kept her distance. She understood that we were as different as the left and the right hand. She knew not to come to me for solutions when her affair went sour like most girls did. I had no shoulders for shedding tears.

I made a decision I wanted to tell Meyer to let her go. I knew, like he did, that he was going nowhere with her. She was not good at looking for opportunities. She would not make use of those that presented themselves and given the chance, she could have done something about her life if she would take the opportunity. She was just a young girl whose leader was her instincts and she followed them with obedience like an animal. He knew all the reasons why she needed to go away, but I wanted to remind him. If he would have taken my mind for granted then I had nothing to lose. While I was figuring out how I would start, he brought it up in one of our talks when he said something about beautiful damsels like Eve after a long yawn.

"I didn't know you thought she was beautiful," I said.

"Who doesn't?"

"Well, if you think she is then you should let her go."

"I have not tied anyone's legs with a rope."

"That's not the point. This girl is...."

"Young and promising with a great future and you think she needs a chance, huh?"

I did not reply. He gave himself a satirical laughter leaving his mouth twisted to one direction.

"I know what you want to do with the young girl," I said.

"You want to impregnate her and then maybe your mission will be complete, right?"

"Give me a break, Brooks. Come on, you should sympathise with me as well. What makes you think age has got anything to do with this? Where do you think I will run away to? I'm a prisoner in it, Brooks Ishimwe, for God's sake. I have nowhere to run."

"Do her a favour by sending her away, Meyer."

"Why can't you do it for me? Go on! Tell her to go. You think I like it with all these girls? I don't keep them coming back. They keep on coming back."

The fruits of our rotten minds came down squeezing bitter juices into the already tattered lives. It looked like everyone had a reason why he failed to do what was right. It flew in our veins and camped in our heads and might not have happened the day which followed or the other but surely it came someday. I was sure that Meyer and his love-girl saw the danger, but I was even more convinced that they did nothing. According to them the commitment of walking away from trouble was more than walking towards it. Our houseboy Tom would have not only have agreed but also would have accepted when he said that life was short and what one needed to do when he came across anything was to put it into his mouth. The first time I stepped into a higher learning institution, what I thought I saw were groups of intelligent people who were role models to the wider society, but I eventually saw that it was quite different. Important decisions and wisdoms of existence did not go beyond a personal level. That's what was meant by saying life was death turned inside out.

There was an old man who claimed to have postponed death in my village. When I heard about it, I did what anybody would have done. I laughed. The man had a terrible dream the previous night that he was drowning, and given his advanced age he associated it with ripe time when he needed to part with life. The following morning tea choked him while he was instructing his granddaughter on how to grind sorghum. The story did not say what he did but he must have spelt out a quick will and asked for forgiveness of his sins. While he was harvesting tobacco down by the river, a cobra basking in the morning sun almost bit him. He gathered courage and cut it into several pieces with a machete screaming at the top of his voice. When the day passed and he did not die, he prayed in his hut every morning asking death to keep away like it did with the cobra and the choke on tea. His belief turned him into a medicine man and people brought him maize and chicken so that he would tell them the day they would die.

While sitting by the fireside at home one day I introduced a topic intentionally to know what other people thought about gender differences. I said that there was no difference between the brains of a man and that of a woman. My stepmother denied quickly, saying men had bigger brains and she said what I had said was lacking respect for them. She gave an example of my father and said that without him everything we had would never have existed and that it was through his wisdom that we managed to grow. Whenever a sensitive issue arose, my stepmother always talked in favour of my father, something I came to know she did out of fear rather than respect. There was that saying that we were growing because of my father, which kept me wondering whether he had an influence over our physical growth. I did not know whether she meant the way we were brought up, but I did not ask because she did not like questions concerning my father. Tom seconded her by faulting my listening skills in the church and found a chance to insult me then when he said I that had received Father Agostinho's award for nothing. He said that even in the Bible stories there was no single woman among the disciples of Jesus. When my sister said that she thought the brains were the same and only the roles differed, my stepmother warned her about such reasoning if she wanted to get married in the future.

They did not give themselves time to think. It was always about the way it was done and if it changed in the way it was believed. There was a common saying among the poor that money and richness was bad. They quoted examples on how they had seen rich people die due to money related problems. It was another way of saying poverty was not a bad thing. In my home village whenever such talk arose they talked about the rich man who had spent years in Canada but was shivering with dogs in the corners of the horticultural market. They were the same people who gave poverty as the chief reason why they were not able to do such and such a thing. They taught their children the same thing without knowing how much they impaired bright futures. It did not occur to me that if I walked down a poor neighbourhood and poured bags of money on the floor, they would enter their houses and close the doors. It was because of such simple utterances that ambitions were shuttered and dreams killed. When I looked at the structure of our family I learnt that speaking ill of progress was one way of justifying the failures of someone in the past.

My grandfather constantly criticized his second born, who spent most of the time making himself drunk in the village. My grandfather never went to school, but surprisingly, he associated alcoholism to illiteracy and irresponsibility. He used to tell me the importance of schooling when I sat between his legs listening to stories. He said that when we went to school he had also gone. He did not seek to justify himself and said that during his time learning was easy, and anyone who was interested in class was given a scholarship to study in England so long as he proved that he was intelligent. He equated the three children, of his second born, who ate at his house, to quadruplets of a goat that were fed on cow milk because their mother was incapable of producing enough and the buck was always away eating grass. He blamed the failures of his sons on lack of an education. Even when my father worked with an environmental conservation programme, what kept him in the position of sample collection were his experience and his ability to communicate in English. He told me that grandfather did not have money for his school fees.

My father had resources and if he wanted to go to school he could have done so without a problem. That was because he was allocated six acres of land and fifteen head of cattle when he was only sixteen. His younger brother, who was allocated three acres, was a civil engineer who taught himself by working hard on his farm. My father was allocated more land because he would break the ground for grandfather's grave as the eldest son. When he came home, his brothers and their wives camped in his compound to eat food and beg for money from him. Sometimes he slaughtered a goat for them during the festive season, and the women cooked it as their children ate incessantly. On such occasions if one wanted to ask the children whether they had eaten enough all he had to do was to ask whether they had been overfed. They never had enough when it came to food. According to my uncles, their brother had money to waste. When he had gone back to the city after a party he threw with intentions of keeping the family united, they gathered to discuss who had eaten more from him.

The scenario women created whenever the man they considered rich was around gave reason as to why people needed compulsory coaching on how they were supposed to behave in a social gathering. They stole raw meat and hid it in the clothes they wrapped around their waists, which served the purpose of restraining wombs tired of giving birth. They disappeared to the back of the house and gave their children, stationed along fences, foodstuffs they looted from the store to take home. There was one who took it a little too far when she hid sugar in one side of her brassier and cooking fat on the other. The sugar fell after she attempted to run when a tethered cow scared her by shaking its long horns. When they felt they had looted enough foodstuffs they stole spoons and plates in turns without suspicion. It would only be known days after when they quarreled and shouted at each other on what they had done. After they overfed themselves they would then burst into song and dance praising the man of the family, telling him that he was good and handsome.

Like my father, it was difficult to meet someone in

the village who said that they used to fail in class. The same way it was difficult to meet someone who said that they had no reason why they never went to school, like my grandfather. They lacked self-acceptance and they would boast on how they calculated mathematics whenever they were called to do so. They were the same people who had problems with addition and subtraction of cash down in the market when selling wares. Much as other people waited to be taught on how to read and write there was nobody who told me and my sister to read and write. We just used to do it because of the joy which came with knowledge. I used to read the *Bible Stories* book because it was the second earliest book at home after the Bible. We used to like it because it had colourful pictures of the stories about David and Goliath, as well as the strength of Samson among others. Because my baby sister did not know how to read, I used to read it then narrate the stories to her. After meals she stood beside me and pestered for a story while sucking on her thumb until I did.

As much as I grew up knowing I had no persuasive authority over anyone or anything or so I was made to believe, I decided to break the chain of slavery and wanted to start it with Meyer's love-girl. I wanted to open her eyes, and if she decided not to accept freedom of sight then she needed to forgive herself for being lost. She was young and promising and Meyer knew that. As much as she was a great ship, the type of leak she considered small would have sunk her forever and that was what I wanted to tell her. She came with a school bag that evening as if she was heeding to a call which could prove who was right between me and Meyer. As it turned out she did not only think I was insane but also strongly believed I was a gross idiot. After we exchanged greetings Meyer signaled me with his eye and smiled with the corner of his mouth then excused himself and walked out. She put her school bag on the table and opened Meyer's wardrobe, then started sorting out his clothes for washing. It was difficult to believe she was on the long direction in her school uniform that always gave a false simplification of wisdom.

"How was your day at school?" I asked her.

"It was good," she said sitting.

She was surprised because I had never asked anything about her.

"Hope it was," I said sitting across the table.

"Sure. Something wrong?" she asked.

"Something is always wrong. It depends on how you think."

I paused to wait for the most persuasive words and simplest language to land in my head.

"And how do I think?"

"I'm afraid wrongly. There is something important I want us to talk about."

"Right away?"

"Yes," I said.

She threw a shirt she was holding into the basin and looked at me. I had her full attention; therefore I did not waste time.

"I do not make decisions for people when they do things which do not affect me directly, but I tell them what I think."

She stared at me.

"You are a young girl and the future is promising. Your relationship with Meyer does not promise much when talking about your future. Without him you have a chance for a future but with him, I'm afraid you are limiting yourself."

"What are you driving at?" she asked, failing to contain her anxiety.

"It's simple. Walk away from him and you will be walking towards a future. He cheats on you when you are not around and he uses you. The difference between you is what you want from each other. You want love and he wants fun. Either, both of you will lose in the long run or he will win."

"I love him," she broke the silence.

If braveness had anything to go by, then Eve was the bravest girl to stand her ground while looking at me in the eyes, after what I had said. She was not surprised, which meant that I had not said anything new to her. It was a strong way of sending a message that she was long decided.

"He is a player," I said without regret.

"I know."

"What?"

"You can call me young or anything you like, but what you should know is that I can think on my own and decide what is right for me."

"If you fall, Meyer will not help you."

"I will not need his help. All boys are players and all men are boys. That is what you and your disciples in the mentoring programme should know, Mr. Elder Chief Advisor. Besides I do not think you know something about relationships. Maybe you should get yourself a girlfriend."

"This is about your life...."

"Good. So stay away from my life."

I obeyed. I knew I could have failed, but I did not know I could have failed with that margin. I did not feel different from one of my principles that guided me all along; I never took blame for what was not my fault. What was in my mind was anger and frustration. She won herself the pride of shutting me up right from the time the conversation started, until it ended like shutting a water tap to the last drop and emptied my mind like the blackout on a prestigious town. When she went away, because she could not stay in the same room as me, Meyer entered and hit my shoulder twice then burst out laughing. He sat on the table and laughed even more when he looked at me. I then felt I had made a grave mistake by diverting a contaminated river in the name of washing it before I left it on its own. I felt I could not even prove the allegations I had made about what the future held for a life I had no business in. The difference between me and Eve was that I had nothing to lose. That was what she did not understand. There were so many schools girls roaming with strangers in the back streets of Thika Road. I did not know why I had chosen to straighten a dry fish in an ocean of shoals.

Tracy reminded me that I needed to do an interview that could make me eligible to participate in the elections of club officials after the third day of the Portuguese week. I had intentions of running for the post of Portuguese president, but after Eve made me feel that I could never successfully advise a high school student, let alone lead a countrywide organisation, I did not only feel incapable but also wanted to drop from it. When I told Tracy my intentions she refused to accept and demanded an explanation. I told her it was personal but when she insisted I broke one of my rules by telling her the story, which was none of her business. She listened carefully and took it lightly, explaining that I did not need to stop vying for an important obligation because a school girl failed to listen to me. Tracy was a stubborn girl when it came to something she believed in. She came to my room to make sure I attended the interview. Later that day I was given the go ahead to interview for the most prestigious position at that time. It could have gone into the history of the language in the country.

Even when I was cleared my spirits were down. I delivered a speech stating reasons as to why the people needed to vote for me as student president, but I noticed that it was not as exciting as that of the opening day. I was prepared to lose as we went about shaking hands and talking nicely to registered members on the material voting day. The competition was stiff as one of the contestants was Fernando Carvalho a former Guinea Bissau citizen, which is a Portuguese speaking country. He had decided to settle in the country after finishing his studies and worked with an information technology company. The voters started voting early that morning on the last day because there were numerous activities like the last days of every event. There was all-night entertainment like the first day and I could see that a large family of different colours and levels had been formed. There was always the craving to make more friends so that they would bring meaning and form reminders of one of the most successful events in the trees and bushes of a well-built city.

After the results were announced I beat a fellow student Eliana by sixteen points and one by fourteen. Carvalho came third with thirteen points. Tracy shouted loudest with pride when I was announced the winner and pinched my ear above cheers. I did not expect to win, and that was what I said in my inauguration speech. I promised to deliver my best and work as a team player with other officials who had been elected to various positions. The lesson I learnt from my win was that the confidence built in the hearts of people whenever they believed in something rarely changed unless an overwhelming evidence arose making them feel they had made a bad decision. They had believed in me and expressed it in the ballot, completing their work. What remained was entirely my part and I was looking forward to it. I remember saying that I would never venture into politics when I was young, but I realised then that it was impossible to achieve some of the dreams without getting a little involved.

I snuck out that afternoon to go and see Adelina. I did not want to go there, but at the same time I did not want her to go the following day without us having one last talk. We had become friends in a full week, which was a long time for a friendship bound to stick. There was something about her politeness which brought with it a unique value. It would not have helped anyone who wanted a jovial person. Adelina's smile came once after a long pause like a season of flowers. Even though, she always looked okay wearing a facial expression that said she was just fine. It needed someone who was very keen to take note that there was undefined sadness behind her casual looking face. I found her preparing a meal while listening to soft Brazilian music. She was happy to see me but I was nervous. For all those days we had spent talking and walking, I never felt free to be myself, even when trust was slowly turning around. With Adelina around, it was like being on holiday; she was the kind of girl who did not spend time trying to change people. Instead, she understood them, picked the few values she could see and moved on from there. I felt a huge relief from the caution of an investigative journalist. In her company I was like any other person.

She insisted that she wanted to stay with the entertainment which had been arranged at the arboretum until daybreak because she did not believe she would have another chance to see the people and friends she had made in a place that only existed in dreams years back. The night was calm when we reached the arboretum; minutes after ambassador Carlito officially closed the event. Tracy had volunteered to serve children with meals and I could tell they liked her as they picked their plates smiling at what she told them. When she saw us, she left her assistant and served two plates then brought them to a table near to where we were standing. We thanked her and she went back to the children. We picked up the plates and walked to wards the trees where we had sat the first day in darkness but I could not tell the exact spot where we sat. Adelina spread down her pullover and we sat down looking to the west. The buildings of the city were hidden except the tallest Kenyatta Conference Centre that stood cylindrically in pride and rudeness.

Adelina sat for a long time staring far beyond the trees. I was aware that sometimes she was lost in memory but that time around it was scary. The spoon she had dug in her food remained stuck there until it became cold from the blowing soft air in the trees. It had become relatively dark in the trees because of the night and the canopy shadows. The night was calm and Adelina was silent. I had thought I knew a few things about her but that night she was different and strange. She tuned off her ears to the sound of the music and the people. Instead, she concentrated on somewhere far. She was not even aware that I was there. Moonlight appeared high in the sky and the stars gathered around it. It was the only sight I knew which annoyed nobody. She collected herself from the deepest memory which was eating her concentration and she took a deep breath. She broke down into a heavy cry which shook her shoulders and heaved her chest. It was difficult to know what to do and even more difficult to know what to say. I turned my eyes towards the bushes.

I knew that trying to be a man was a priority for anyone who wanted a higher self-esteem like me, while getting noticed was the pride of any young woman, like Adelina. I had not spent time studying how people behaved and why for nothing. I was aware that on most occasions, women saw themselves more in terms of relationships and men regarded themselves in terms of what they did. When that did not work for the women it resulted in emotions but for men it developed in anger and frustration. That night, Adelina was crying because of different reasons that I did not even fully understand. That made it even more complicated for me. I did not know whether becoming a man included comforting a new friend who considered me a stranger. If that was the examination then I did not need to be told that I had failed. That did not mean I did not feel for her. I did know how to put that into words, so I knew I had already made an ass of myself. I think I would have made a very bad social worker.

She was beautiful and delicate even when she was in tears. She might have had family problems but her success and the distance she had come did not seem to make her feel important. Having grown and fumbled for the way forward on my own, after my mother's demise, I did not know which was better between having both parents who stayed apart without the likelihood of ever coming together and having one or both who died. Somebody needed to pick the pieces and move forward. Someone needed to understand that it was not their fault that what was happening in their lives did happen. I wanted to tell Adelina all those things but I did not know how to put them into words. I looked at her teary eyes of innocence and felt it in my nerve. The air grew thicker and my throat dried from the saliva that I could not secrete. That night I was not Brooks, the investigative journalist, but a civilian who did not know what to do and when. I felt like a drowning man who was fumbling for something to hold onto.

"You will get over it," I said with a clogged voice.

"You will just be fine." I added.

With those two simple sentences, she cooled down and looked at me. She moved closer and put her head on my chest. I put my arm around her. She turned her eyes to the orange horizon and blinked once then closed them. She then lit her face with the smile of assurance like the moon lit the sky. The ground ants which had discovered the food on her plate were busy eating and inviting many others underground. With her eyes still closed she felt for her plate and turned it upside down drowning the ants which had gathered for a feast. She shook off one ant that clung on her hand and then crossed her hands across her chest like a sleeping child. Once again she was Adelina; the polite girl who wore a beautiful, casual face. She was the simple girl who refused to wear the lenses of magnifying what other people were bad at. There was something different about that night as the party went on and more people poured to the dancing space.

"Can we spend some time dancing tonight?" She asked.

"Sure," I said without room to object.

The stars stayed in place competing to produce light. Smaller ones joined them and as the clock ticked into the night, the sky was alive with thousands of stars that chased away the clouds and kept the moon in company. They started playing games by making great dashes across the sky towards the south, and I knew the morning of another day was not far away.

Chapter Eight

Mrs. Fabiano congratulated me for being elected for the position of the club president. She insisted that I needed to be in a guidance counseling community service programme in schools along Thika Road. She picked me from class that morning to do a hurried paper examination even though I had not attended the three day workshop that was initiated by an organisation on behavioural change. I did not object because she picked someone whenever she saw need and always had reasons for doing so. I was picked among a few others from a large number which had turned out for the examinations. The programme attracted many because it had good allowances and a heavy salary at the end of the exercise, which was very important for anyone who had tasted the life of being a college student. Recommending someone familiar when in good terms was the hardest task one could have been given, but Mrs. Fabiano always found it easy with openness and honesty. She was a real woman who always spared rights for devils and rights for angels. That was reason enough to have confidence that even when she recommended me as one of the selection panel, I deserved it.

I doubted the validity of Mrs. Fabiano's approval whenever she wanted me to do something. It seemed to me that she came to believe I was good in everything. She did not know that I had failed on my first attempt to show someone the way. Walking out there to convince youngsters was not as easy as it looked. They were in their vital stages of development where observation and experiment worked more in their lives than the lectures that we were assigned to deliver. Experience was crucial in such an assignment even when it raised little or no concern from the organizers. In my job, I had witnessed what people did and unearthed mysteries in which I started with a very simple variable than anyone thought important and ended up with a chain of events which left people with their mouths wide open. Even though, I understood that it did not mean I could produce remedies to the same problems that I found out. A person could discover an insect but that did not mean he or she could discover its insecticide. I did not know whether I would make enemies or friends with the kids. I had seen it with Eve, someone with whom I did not think I would ever become friends.

Unlike inexperienced people like me, Professor Nairit had a lot of experience with youngsters and I could tell their way of life did not impress him, which was the reason why he was always in conflict with those he tried to teach how to lead good lives, according to him. I knew that when giving information to young people, first of all you needed to make sure they liked you. When telling them about a fact they did not like, one needed to have sufficient information to pass out the point. If that did not happen then dislike came about that easily changed to hatred. That was what Nairit did not do, and therefore he not only became a victim of hatred but also an asset of disrespect. When Haamid had arrived, the old man seemed to have cooled down and he started developing peace within himself. With his son close to him, he often smiled and his nose seemed to have grown longer, especially when he was laughing. The stretch of his mouth in laughter made it look like the tusk of a baby elephant.

Professor Nairit called me to his house one

evening, and I began to think something serious had happened. It was difficult to think about something positive in a meeting with him. We usually discussed the issues of the mentoring programme in his office and he would then give me something to do for him if he needed it. I respected his call and went to his compound. There were three gates opening to the inner compound and I noticed that the gatekeepers had instructions of keeping them shut immediately after someone entered. I found him walking around his botanical garden, which had beautiful flowers and other plants. When he saw me he signaled a worker who was watering them, to go away.

"How has your day been, young blood?" he asked.

He used to call someone 'young blood' whenever he meant to be polite.

"It was good, sir," I replied.

He moved near a bunch of roses and plucked one then smelt it. He closed his eyes and took a breath.

"You know life is not so bad, young blood. It is a matter of choices. Some people make wrong choices while some make good choices, but there are those who do not have choices at all, and that is where most people pretend they belong."

He looked at his watch and ground his teeth then started walking along the hedge of the flowers. I followed him.

"What I'm saying is that there are many reasons as to why people do things the way they do. Some behave the way they do because of fear and come out smiling because whatever they have done is considered acceptable given the way it has been made to look and not the way it is."

He paused to look at me and all of a sudden his

face changed.

"I have not called you to tell you about what I think, nor have I called you to say that you are that different. It is very difficult to notice the difference in the way of this generation, but sometimes a farmer can decide to pick an edible fruit from rotten ones when counting the losses of his work."

The old man who never believed there was a single person in the changing world who would have been as good as his young times had called me to tell me what was on his mind. He looked unmoved and was fully aware that most young people did not like his ways. They might have shouted at the top of their voices and called him 'the kilogramme' or whatever they wanted, but he was not willing to adjust himself for the world simply because change had called for it in a way he described as "for the worse". He was pleased with himself and what he had achieved. He was a man who marked his own life examination and gave himself recommendations. He was happy whenever he mentioned Haamid and the countable hairs on his bald head seemed to be growing fewer.

"Haamid is good, right?"

"Yes he is," I said.

He gave himself an old smile and rubbed his cheek in pride.

"My life is considered over but I can say it has just begun." He looked at the direction of the setting sun and ground his teeth. He thought for a while and then turned towards me with an angry face.

"There are so many ways of telling someone that you believe in them. You can tell them that by giving them duties and when they are young their job is to obey."

He stopped then stared at me.

"You rejected my appointment to a position in which I believed you would have performed well."

I opened my mouth to protest but he waved it away.

"I understand," he said.

He put his arm around me.

"But you are good and so is Haamid."

They were words which someone would have never expected from someone like Professor Nairit. Those who knew him would have agreed that he was one person who did not have a hundred percent commendation on anything. One would have been certain the word 'but' always followed his appreciation. Whenever he saw someone had done something in the right way he just kept quiet and that was the best he would provide. Otherwise most of the times he concentrated on mistakes and whenever he failed to get any he looked for them. He was a person who confined himself to his own way of operation which was difficult to copy. I did not know then whether he was serious with what he had said nor did I know what he would have added next, but one thing I understood very well was that one did not need to fool himself with Nairit because he was a person who would have cried at the end of a laughing.

"You know, inside there they think I'm an idiot," he said, pointing in the direction of the hostels.

"Ever seen people who think collectively but wrongly?"

I did not know what to say so I laughed.

"When you meet them tell them, and show them what they are supposed to do. Maybe they will respect your membership of their generation."

It was not that there was any difference between

talking to a young or older person when he was speaking his mind. It was rumoured that he was always in conflict with the senate whenever he was called to account for the performance of his students during the annual meetings. Effective teaching was supposed to reflect an *ogive* curve when total results were expressed graphically, but when he was called upon to explain why his was producing different results, he usually had funny reasons that sent members of the meeting into laughter. At one time he became agitated when the academic registrar asked why most of his students had failed in a unit the previous semester.

"I do not know," he said.

"Maybe you brought me fools."

On the morning of the first day of community work, as the school buses were roaring at the parking lounge, I made short notes on what I intended to say having been allocated children of less than seven years. The best way I worked whenever I inspired myself was not to accept excuses for failing to do something. I had made a decision that I wanted to nurture their ability to think on their own, which was what I did with Russel from the time he was very young. I also wanted to learn some things from them and this was the way I spent my time in anything I did. I would have preferred a routine check on how the kids were doing and what they thought about our talk days after, but it looked like that was not going to be a possibility.

I understood that even when we said "so far so good", it was not good enough until we were either on top or side-by-side with everyone which I knew was not easy. The tallest pillars, like professor Nairit, did not see its possibility and their experience was not something to underrate. According to him, it was time people needed to examine whether they were edible fruits in piles of rotten ones. That was the basis of progress, which was not dependent on the step we had made but how willing we were to make another one. It did not matter anymore how best one imitated but how efficiently he used his brain. The difference in generation came with great changes, and everyone thought their times were the best times. During one of my grandfather's memorial parties, a man shared a cigarette with his six-year-old son, just to show how much he loved him. He even went ahead explaining that the boy was part of him and resembled him in everything, including his smoking habits.

Although I admit that I was left on my own which was why I learnt things on my own, I realised that those before us did not teach us to adjust to the changing times. My stepmother believed that a young man should not have gone beyond twenty years without getting married. When I asked her why she believed like that she said it was the way it was from the past which was admirable. To her, there was no such a thing as a woman of dreams, about whom we spent nights thinking and waiting for so long. She forgot that in the past, marriages went hand-in-hand with inherited wealth, which a person used to settle down when bringing up a family. The great changes in population trends and modern times had buried all that in an irretrievable grave. The lands were badly fragmented;   parents warned their children working on them not to dig on each other's backs.

The same way all people were afraid of change, parents were always nervous of a foreign trend. They preferred the way they were brought up. With many days of observation, I realised that they were even afraid of material wealth because they were brought up in poverty. There was that belief in rural areas that towns had all the necessary evil a person needed before he burnt in hell. They were ready to discredit anything from those places as soon as they heard about or saw it. One day when my stepmother came and found me speaking English with my little sister, she called it town nonsense and said she did not want to hear about it in the house. She gave an example of a man who started the same thing in the village and was lynched by a mob in one of the slums she did not even know. My little sister started laughing and asked her why they learnt it as a compulsory subject in class. When she failed to reply, I walked away to avoid sharing the embarrassment.

There were situations where what existed previously would have never applied. It was all about thinking and that was what people did not do. When I was young I had a problem managing my anger. One day I clubbed to death a new-born calf because it refused to enter its room and kept on jumping up and down in darkness. As usual, my father had no reserved comments in something like that. He just spoke a few words about how I was a bad example to my younger sister and kept quiet. The real wrath came from my stepmother. She made me dig the grave and say a prayer before burying the calf. She then put me into a milk drinking drought for two years; until the cow had another calf. I had thought she had forgotten but kept on asking for forgiveness on my behalf in the prayer before we went to bed. From that day on, I usually took my time to cool down whenever something offended me until I would resolve to something better and I saw what independent thinking did for me.

When my cousin from my youngest uncle luckily got a job in a security firm as a gate keeper in Nairobi, after dropping out of school he got married as expected, of course, and brought home a woman from town. I did not know why the minds of people with little education surrounded marriages and children. That evening, women, even strangers, were on the fences to see what she looked like because they had nothing else to do. They even volunteered to help his mother weed her garden the following day so that they would see her and gossip with their friends in numerous versions. They monitored her movements and were keen to note whether she would light firewood in the smoky kitchen and make food with the traditional three stones. They yearned to shake her hand to feel whether it was a 'hand of work' by which they meant it should have been hard textured. They did not prefer soft hands in the village because they brought up complaints about calluses when working in farms. They considered those women from town as soft and delicate people who would not grind sorghum using stone.

The kids were delighted to see us in our first school. They greeted us with two hands as a virtue of respect and were eager to listen to what we were telling them. It never occurred to me that they would have so much respect for us and recognition that they treated us like elders of wisdom. When I was given my group under the tree, I did what I used to see our Sunday school teachers do when talking to us. I knelt down so that they would feel I was one of them and become free. They asked many questions, some of which were technical and needed time to answer. I posed questions to them to test their intelligence and I could see that those young kids were more observant and knowledgeable than they were thought to be.

"As children we should be wary of bad habits as we grow up," I told them.

"What are some of the bad habits?"

A boy raised up his hand.

"Scratching private parts in public."

The others laughed.

"Any others?"

"Drinking and smoking," a girl said.

"What do people who smoke and drink do?" I asked her.

"They do not take showers," a little boy of about four said.

I told the others to pave him a way so that he could come to the front and sit by my side.

"What else do they do?" I asked him.

He thought for a while before he replied.

"They beat their wives."

I knew that what those children were saying was a reality they had seen somewhere at that stage when observation was the most critical mode of learning. They had a wonderful sense of interpretation and a burning set of ideas, and their young brains were a wonderful and never ending resource. I, as well, knew that some of them became what they saw. They modeled themselves after their parents and their teachers, and they gave me a variety of answers when I asked them what they wanted to be in future. Some said engineers like their fathers or nurses like their mothers. Even when I gave them a lot of time to exhaust their lists, I realised that there was no single one of them who wanted to be a teacher. The deputy principal scribbled it in her notebook and shook her head.

We became good friends because as time went by, the kids became more confident and asked what was on their minds. They knew many things and understood the mysteries behind them, compared to those in the countryside who woke up every day to see only animals and bushes then maybe crops. I remember a boy in his first year in high school who was asked by a dormitory wag what the colour of a television looked like, and to my surprise, he had no idea. We were lucky to have some of those privileges in our family and we could learn what the outside world was doing through news and documentaries. When I was finishing I told them to ask any questions. There was that little girl who sent me walking on a tight rope when I gave her the go ahead. Some of them already knew the answer because they started laughing.

"I know that children come from the belly but what I do not know is.....how do they get there?"

That afternoon I shifted classes with Tracy who went to be in charge of the kids as I took on teenagers in the next school. There was nothing which excited her more nor had I seen her as happy any other day than when I saw her that afternoon. She had looked for an opportunity to be near children all her life and her chance had come. She would have jumped up and down like the troublesome calf. She rubbed her hands and waved me away from the direction of the kids who were settling under the giant tree.

"Do you know what I do with excited calves?" I joked.

"Excuse me?" she asked above the noise.

I had told her the story but I could see that she did not remember. We walked some distance away from the bus as the teachers and organisers were busy directing pupils from one hall to the other.

"The cow is almost calving down," she said.

I laughed.

"When I'll walk under that tree," she pointed to the direction with her forefinger.

"I will be standing in front of a large children's home telling them why they are the most important people in the world."

"If you stray away from the purpose of the trip they will fire you before evening."

"I've not come here to work for them but to give children the ability to define life even in the middle of a horrible dream."

When she looked at me and saw me doubt the wisdom of what she wanted to do, she shrugged.

"Wait and see," she said and turned her head towards the afternoon sun.

There was a wide belief that children were a blessing from a supreme being. That was why during those times, when my father was still a teenager, it was a taboo to question the numbers of those who were born. They left it to chance and believed such questioning would have led to barrenness somewhere along the line. My comic grandfather used to tell me that a true man sired children until he got fed up. He would then lower his head thinking and add that largely it was because in those days, women worked hard in the farms to fend for the families. The work of men was just supervision and technical advice whenever it was needed. He would then laugh briefly and talk about how men carried children on their backs to clinics while their wives strolled besides them claiming they were tired in the modern times, then boast that he never held my father in his hands more than the day he was born because he needed to show him to the rising sun for blessings and health.

Tracy seemed to agree with those who lived before us. If she did not agree then she did not know what she thought about it. She was not interested in the threat of a population trend but the lives of children which were largely influenced by the way they were raised. It was not that I expected much from a girl who just happened in the streets. Humanity took the larger part of her reasoning and she lost a reverse gear to look at other dimensions when it came to talking about children. That was why I got myself into trouble with her the day I stupidly joked that making children in the streets comfortable would have encouraged more pouring in. She was the same as the son in the story of a girl who came home and found her father being beaten by a mob for stealing a sack of maize and then was torn between rescuing the father and letting justice take its course, and the son who rushed to rescue his father and said he did not know about the theft.

I felt saddened when I looked at the high school teenagers entering the hall. I had decided I was not going to write any short notes, and whenever I felt like that I obeyed because I would not have referred to them. I knew what I wanted to tell them once I stepped into that hall. They were the bright faces of the future behind which intelligent brains of numerous expectations lay. They were ready to learn and smiled to the joy of knowledge each time they discovered something new. Their minds were geared towards success in everything they did, from their dressing to the way they spent their time. Their lives never ended the way they looked at that stage. Years after, there would be a Meyer or an Irene somewhere and very few ended up like Tracy, while others would live with regret in their advanced ages like professor Nairit. There was somewhere in between a transitional stage where the intelligence system broke down.

As it would have been expected, the teenagers were keen on how I dressed and absorbed each word, then digested it within themselves to see its relevance to what they had gathered there. Their age and status made them have a difficult time, restraining them from their choices for role models in what they thought were lifetime dreams such as those of joining campus and becoming peer counsellors like us. They clapped when I entered that hall which took me to a memory years back, when we used to receive visitors in school. There were no counsellors back then, but we did receive numerous self-proclaimed prophets who scared us out of our minds with noises about exaggerated fire theories which we talked about many days after.

"All of you will agree with me that you look so amazing." I started.

They clapped but I would see it was out of procedure rather than appreciation.

"It would have been more amazing if tomorrow and the day after you look like this. Does that happen? Of course not. There are a number of reasons as to why some of you might look the way you do today. You dress well and keep time as well as read because either your teachers tell you to do so or it is what you think students should do. It does not come from within yourselves," I began.

"As it happens a number of you will change completely soon after high school. I'm not talking about the physical changes but the psychological ones that are either building or destroying you even right now. I can hear them calling for cement and bricks."

They laughed and thought it was very funny.

"I want us to look at some time before or after the eighteenth birthday. It is within us and we know it, yet we do not want to see it. I want you to look at people you know who are now out of school. Do they look similar to the way they were when they were like you?"

I saw them look into air and then register a solid proof, then believe what I told them by becoming more attentive and looking at me. The whispers at the back died down and there was silence.

"There are a few things that can make people change for the better or worse. You will realise that when you finish high school. There will be no teachers to tell you when to wake up, no bells and no punishments. All decisions are made by you, and that is where simple chromatography begins; the great separation of people into different colours of their lives that put them at an advantage or a disadvantage for eternity. Those who choose to do wrong do so because they think they will look greater than the rest and those with the ability to use their brains proceed to great heights. The more you grow the more you are left to become independent but nobody will tell you that. How can you do this? It's simple. The ability to think overcomes everything, and it is the only thing I find amusing."

I paused to let them digest what I had said.

"I want you to think of two boys sitting in the same class as this one. The first boy sags his trouser and tucks in only when the teacher is around. He spends his time by flirting with girls and some fall into his trap. He might say one or two rude words to a teacher to look bigger. He starts pointless fights to gain supremacy and can puff a cigarette smuggled in here or sip an alcoholic drink, then tell everyone what he has done. The same boy folds the test paper as soon as the teacher gives it to him to hide his score."

I paused to let them settle down because they had started laughing and summing up what I said to the people they knew.

"Years later, the boy is in the village with broken teeth as a result of his fighting and splitting firewood for brewers to get local brew for his thirst. He is dirty and smelling because he sees nothing wrong with it. He will have hungry children who dress barely beyond their hips. He will complain about being abandoned by his learned brothers and sisters who have jobs, not knowing he wasted his time."

The smiling faces turned to sadness then anger which brought with it creases at the top of their faces. I knew all the time they had seen the characters I was talking about in the streets and in the neighbourhoods where they came from. There was that habit of getting used to something until one forgot its implication or harmfulness. Like a small child who is first scared with a baby snake, and then as time goes by he moves nearer until he touches it then remembers the first precaution when it bites him. The difference between what they did right and what they thought they did right was that they did not take time to learn from them and that was why I stood before them that day.

"The second boy puts his brain into gear before doing anything. His self-esteem is built by his success and he does not need to be praised to do the right thing. He does not read when the teacher says so and thinks about the value of something before he engages in it. The fact that the first boy mocks him does not affect his performance in anything."

They started clapping.

"He is the kind of boy who gets a nice job years later and owns expensive cars and property. He brings up a happy family and does not depend on anyone."

Somewhere in a public talk, the participation of the audience was required. I paused again and directed a question to them.

"What am I talking about?" I asked.

I saw hands shoot up almost immediately. I picked a girl who was near the dais.

"We should use our brains to differentiate between what is right and wrong," she said, and then nodded her head to show that it had all sunk into her memory.

They were clever minds who would have transformed the entire continent if the status of their minds would have been maintained or improved. The problem was not themselves, but the ability to know that. They did not know that they were important enough to bring changes and that it started within them. The ability to know they were long-term solutions was the real obstacle which stuffed them into the category of wasted resources.

"The same way I have talked about two boys there are two girls as well." I said.

I saw the girls cross their arms and become attentive and listen to themselves and their hearts then judge on which side they belonged.

"The first girl is beautiful and she knows it. Boys approach her who she considers assets and does not want to lose. To maintain them coming back, she has a lot of make up in her drawer and applies lip gloss every twenty minutes. Her wardrobe overflows with new clothes and expensive foodstuffs. Her mouth is always chewing but she sleeps on her desk fifteen minutes after opening a book."

They started laughing.

"She is the type who comes from holidays pregnant, and when she is sent away she opts to get married in the village or by some casual labourer in the streets as a shortcut to rectify her regrets. She is not in control of her life and that is why she sires many children who automatically become a burden."

"What happens after that?"I asked.

I heard a variety of answers from going back to her parents to roaming around homesteads which meant they had seen it happen.

"She roams from one house to the other, a child strapped to her back and two others walking beside her, to see if she can wash clothes and clean compounds in the neighbourhood to get few shillings for food. If she is in the village, she walks to people's farms to pick tea and weed their crops for little money to buy food, and that becomes an occupation throughout her life."

Their hands were to their cheeks then.

"The second girl is on her books. She is interested in boys when competing on performance. Her happiness is success and she does everything in the right way. She works hard and goes to college then graduates with great honours, which secures her a nice job. She gets married to a learned man and her children look healthy all the time."

I saw some boys look to the direction of the girls. A couple of them laughed when their eyes met.

"It depends on you. The cycle of a good or bad life is your ability to think. The answers do not come from anybody other than you. Nature only permits life and death. There are no intermediates. The only thing in between is your brain. Your ability to think is the distance between life and death."

Chapter Nine

The girl on the next block was singing a song at the top her lungs, which penetrated the adjacent blocks and beyond. It would have sent snakes coiling and disappearing into their holes. The well-defined irritating sound found its way into sleeping ears and cut dreams short by a forced vibration of the ear drums. It was as if the sound wanted to prove that dreams were always incomplete. Beds creaked from the rooms as people turned themselves in different directions and clicked to confirm they did not like it. A few unbolted their doors noisily and dragged their feet on the floor to the toilets at the far end. The girl was not moved and went on singing, tearing into people's nerves at such an odd hour when sleep was said to be sweetest. Had I been asked my opinion, I would have recommended that she seek a psychological examination. She was washing clothes on the balcony past midnight when she was supposed to be asleep. She was always washing clothes that I doubted whether she wore because the only way of recognising her from a distance was through seeing a white striped track suit that she never took off.

Robbers walking in between the two buildings had successfully broken into a third shop and were on their way to a get-away lorry hidden behind an adjacent building, away from light and discovery. The night was dark and the compound was lit by the mercy of the generator that roared to life after a major blackout, which left the whole place at the mercy of

God, except in expensive compounds towards the horizon. Along Thika Road almost everything was an advantage, and robbers as well as muggers were celebrating that night. They made stealing a game, to the extent a person knew his property had been vandalized but never dared to raise a complaint. He would wait for the day which followed to plan on how to recover the loss by the same method. The people not only knew the rules but also followed them. That was why it would have been helpless to shout because nobody would have come to rescue them. It was considered a stupid risk which sent the hare hanging from the trap. So the robbers stole with minimum interference, and whenever they found someone they even exchanged greetings.

The mosquitoes which had gone on a rampage prevented me from finishing a book I was reading using the security light, which was dim from an accumulation of insect droppings. They seemed to have been released by an alien from a distant planet, and their aim was not biting to suck but to make sure that nobody enjoyed anything at that hour which was associated with the darkness. Blood or no blood, they were always as thin as a cobweb thread. One would have seen their intestines from the outside of their translucent bodies but they never died of hunger. I slapped my arm to scare some away because trying to kill a Thika Road mosquito was an exercise in futility. The tap in the toilet was loose and the water kept dropping on the floor noisily at the time of the night when a small sound went far. The sound was not heard during the early hours, but as it hit the toilet floor it sounded as if someone was hammering something in the sleeping neighbourhood. The blackout had messed up those men who had tendencies of playing music throughout the night so that they could discourage never-ending talks about family problems from their wives.

The girl resumed from a hum and filled her lungs then released another scream across the block and beyond, sending the dogs in the neighbourhood barking in a well-coordinated alarm that split them into groups and made them bark at intervals. They drowned out the sound of a mongrel from the next compound, which had a poor sense and only relied on the other dogs to follow suit. It would then bark like a lung patient until the three-legged cat diverted its attention or until its vocal cords stopped producing sound. Gangsters had raided the compound several times and tied the watchman to a tree, then carried everything they thought was valuable with minimum interference from the mongrel. It would then be seen in the morning with his tail between his legs walking around the owner as he explained what had happened the previous night to police on patrol, who recorded the statements yawning with tired and fed up faces. Like many cases, nothing much would be done about the robbery because they were numerous, day and night, making them impossible to follow.

Unlike the dog in the next compound, the girl next door had no sense at all. She did not know how to differentiate between night and day or darkness and light. The most irritating part was that she did not sense at all that there were people around her that needed the silence that she was not ready to provide, even at such an hour when everyone needed rest if any work was going to be done the following day. Even when they got annoyed of her, there was nobody who ever asked her why she was born to disturb other people. They swelled their cheeks and clicked in anger but went on with their work because they thought it was none of their business. There were some ladies who incited her to make more noise by forging a conversation and then she would be heard laughing like many clinking glasses. One of those days I wanted to walk across there and speak my mind.

The stars had moved away from the moon to the east, like disobedient children making fun of a man abandoned at old age. The dark clouds, which were constantly moved by air currents, prevented it from providing enough light below, creating partial darkness to the direction the clouds were moving. Night birds sped towards the west in twos, chasing insects and eating them. They were making it a competitive game more than just a food chain. It was difficult not to think about demons when looking at the buildings towards the second lecture hall which looked like ghosts and the shadows of the trees around them like their servants. As a matter of fact, the compound towards that direction was dead on sight. Two stray dogs sped across the grass chasing the three-legged cat, which roared and climbed the wall making them look foolish. They threatened it with a few barks, then went on their way looking for something to eat.

Someone was paying dearly for careless eating in the toilet. He was yelling like a defecating dog that had spent the previous day eating bones. He mumbled something incomprehensible then sealed it with a soft whistle to tell anybody or anything listening at that time that he was okay. The dripping water from the loose tap kept hitting the floor as if the night did not need complete silence. The girl had gone silent and I hoped that something would send her inside the room to sleep. As she gave me and everything else a moment of relief, a drunken man across the road was shouting at the top of his lungs. He called all muggers of Thika Road telling them to go and rob him of a huge amount of money he was carrying. Even when he was not visible in the darkness, I knew he was some toothless fellow wearing a dirty jacket and bathroom slippers of different colours, whose torn strings had been mended by pieces of a wire stolen from a barbed fence. He was one of those characters who was never in places for nothing but always in the places for something.

The watchman towards the second gate stirred into life after he had spent time on his chair drunk from as early as eight o'clock. He had stayed there not aware of himself with his mouth open and saliva falling across his cheek. He touched his head in search of his duty cap and when he did not find it there, he looked around and found it on the grass and put it on. The mosquitoes must have feasted on his shaved head. He scratched it severally to soothe numerous holes they had drilled in it, then he reached under the chair and fished a hidden bottle of liquor. He emptied it and threw it down, then strolled towards the back of the lecture hall hoping to find everything okay. A naked girl opened the door from the opposite male hostel block and tried to run downstairs. A boy came out and stopped her. They argued for a time with the girl throwing up her hands; finally, he took her inside. The three-legged cat jumped from the rubbish bin when they were gone with the bone of a fish. There was plenty of food for those stray animals. All they had to do was to sniff it out. They had more plenty of basic needs than the people who owned them.

Those who were working were aware that the date of the month was twenty something and the accumulated debts had already reached half the salary, which was still days away. The banks were on their necks demanding payment of their loans and they had started clearing anything in the accounts without consultation. Thieves passed with anything on their way because their families needed to eat too. Everybody and everything turned hostile. From street boys who spared nobody when they were hungry to hand-to-mouth dependents who thought those who were supposed to feed them had found other ways of spending their money. They had a hard time giving unwanted explanations to their relatives back at home who demanded to be told how they would survive until the salary was received. What was interesting was that they were the same people who were busy making merry years before, when others were struggling to make better lives. Those who had something to do lived in more misery than those who did nothing at all because the lives they prepared to improve years before were torn by expectations and responsibilities.

Relatives from both sides of couples waited for their pockets like the Israelites did for Manna, convinced that feeding and making them happy was a responsibility. They created more problems for themselves every day and sired many children even at advanced stages, then expected those who had jobs to take care of their large families. There was always news from the countryside that someone had fought or stolen and money was needed to pay for their fines. They were on phones every day, complaining they needed financial assistance, and whenever their desires were not met, they told everyone who was willing to listen that their blood brothers and sisters had abandoned them. With time they transformed the hand they were given from a privilege to a right which needed honour. There was the story of a school dropout who received three thousand shilling in his account every month from his working brother in the capital to buy food for his family. One day, when he received two thousand shillings, he refused to accept the money and until his brother made them three.

Such was the scene one woke up to in the countryside. Men woke up daily to the roadsides, not to look at newspapers because they could not read, but to catch some political and village gossip so that they would talk about it while playing draft the whole day. They would talk about some people in the village who had made it and managed to build executive houses or own expensive vehicles, then share views about how they ignored their brothers and sisters who long went parallel with education by dropping out of school to marry or get married and suffer struggling lives. To them, success was defined in terms of luck. They argued that if someone managed to get his hands in a bee hive, then all he needed to do was to throw down the honey. They would then talk about corruption in the cabinet which sat miles away and argue on which patterns to vote in an election which was four years to come. As it happened, they went away in the evening without an agreement to continue with the talk the day that followed. They would argue forever and what took them back to their houses was to beat their wives for imaginary mistakes if they failed to see any.

There was a linguistics professor from the department of German who told me a real life story, which stayed in my mind for many days, after I commented in admiration of a delegate who arrived driving a Mercedes Benz when we met during the annual language day Anniversary at the main hall. He drove a Toyota Prado and was in an expensive suit, but he was eating two slices of bread and juice

173

for lunch in his vehicle. I refused to accept it when he said that I had more money than him, referring to the pocket money of a student because he did not know that I was working. He gave me a breakdown of the way his salary disappeared into loopholes, and if what he confessed was true, then people needed to diversify their economy before group revolutions materialise. He earned one hundred twenty thousand shillings, but his two children and his four brothers in school needed two times that amount each term. His sister-in-law had added up to the number and yet he needed to pay rent, water and electricity bills then put food on the table among other expenses before thinking about fuelling his luxury vehicle.

While other people saw hardship as an advantage to work and improve their lives, the people who paraded their legs on benches along roads spent time looking for anyone who made it to the top to extract money from them because, as they argued, people earned a lot of money which had no use as they only fed some two little kids. They would arrive in cities, before the cock crowed, with small sacks of green bananas and sorghum, then camp in the houses until something sent them back to the village. They always thought the things such people owned lacked use and cleared refrigerators when they were away at work before disturbing the neighbourhood with music systems. When they were sent back to the countryside after becoming unbearable, they blamed it on the mothers of the houses and accused their husbands for not acting, causing quarrels and break ups of previously peaceful families. They would then celebrate back in the villages for blunt curses they made that the marriages would not last.

Whenever stupid people failed to succeed, they thought those with success were the cause of their failure in one way or another. They would see their rise as unfair because it was not uniform, and the thought led to hatred. They then gathered in groups telling each other that people were never buried with vehicles and bungalows. They would cite death as an ultimate end which did not honour status and long for the day the successful people died in their talks, swearing they would never be part of their burial. There was such a boy who said that to me, but when I asked him, who was likely to die first between the rich and the poor like him, he had no idea. He was one of those people who sent his children to his mother's kitchen during lunch time and disappeared until it was dark and safe enough for the night. Such people and their children used shopping meant for parents that was sent by their hard-working brothers and sisters. They sent their children to occupy the rooms of the houses built for their parents and argued that the rooms did not have any other use.

I used to think it was a farce but some men disappeared when their wives were about to deliver and reappeared after their parents had settled maternal bills. It happened in marriages far away from the common scenarios and in youth relationships where whenever a girl fell pregnant she was on her own. But in a place like Thika Road the women knew better. In times like those of the night termination of pregnancies which took place in houses covered by darkness. The self-proclaimed doctors who were apologetically paperless made thousands of shillings from the activity whose main customers were underage teenagers. It would never be heard until tragedy happened, and tragedy was not tragedy until it was exposed in the news for public scrutiny. The exercise would then be postponed for some time before it emerged again in different places. The night had secrets which would have shocked people to death if only it would speak. I was aware of this fact when I looked into the darkness beyond the capital, whose evidence of existence in such an hour was kept alive by a few shining roofs from a dim light in the distance.

The clouds towards the west were pregnant and stagnant for a long time, forming a red gathering in the sky where the sun had disappeared from the late hours of the previous day. There were still private vehicles on the road with flickering red indicators. I did not like the colour because the sight always sent precaution down to the deepest of my senses. I always wondered why red was called a romantic colour. I did not ask myself questions because they were for people in love and love was something I was yet to understand. In the meantime, it was a scary colour which I always associated with things I did not like: warning street lights, butchery colours, and the shed of blood and danger signals. The sky changed from bright orange to red with time making it look as if the road towards hell was towards that direction. Those who thought below the waist line would have said something different.

Full moon appeared, lighting the earth below. It had managed to chase away the clouds and boasted with the richness of light to show who the boss in the outer space was. The brightness made long and dark shadows from structures that looked overlapped and crossed, making the area below them look like a demonic grapevine farm. The security officer, who had gone to inspect the hall came out satisfied that everything was intact. He took out a paper from the pocket and started rolling a joint. When he was done he lit it and started smoking. His female counterpart, in charge of the maintenance house, saw him smoke and advanced, knocking her behind lightly with a truncheon. They talked a little, after which she took the joint from him and smoked too. They teased each other for some time then chased each other and disappeared behind the hall.

Something appeared from the left corner along the fence. It was as white as cotton wool and shone with the light off the moon. From a distance it looked like a paper bag that had, by some miracle, escaped from one of the rubbish collection pits, which were well built to prevent wind from blowing rubbish out. As it advanced I could see then that it was a person walking along the fence. Security guards did not wear uniforms of that colour and I wondered what a person would do along a fence at such an odd hour. I did not believe angels could exist along Thika Road either. Maybe devils, but the devil had nothing to do with white colours. It was a little after two o'clock in the morning and before long cocks in the distance would start crowing. As the person advanced, I could see that it was a girl. Maybe one who was running away from a love gone sour.

Sleep, which had begun distorting my sight, disappeared as the girl stopped and looked towards the horizon. She touched the wall fence and caressed it as if it was a pillow. She was out of her mind because of reasons that were not easy to guess correctly, given that so many things happened at that hour of the night. There was the possibility that she had been forced into the cold by drug use. I would not have been surprised after I found a group of girls smoking pot in the playing field and chuckling like monkeys on holiday. The efforts of those who campaigned against drugs were fast proving futile. They needed to reshuffle their approaches each day to try and reduce the large numbers of users which swelled like seconds on the wall clock. The youths who were power houses of the nation had been reduced to bone structures with useless minds which had long lost their sense of time or purpose. Interestingly more recruited themselves into the category and it did not take long to see how their lives ended. There was a boy who used to smoke and drink in school and as expected he failed his examinations. When he became a dependent of his own cause he found me one day coming from inspecting our farm and said he needed three shillings for a cigarette. I simply told him to work for his cigarette money.

When the girl turned her face towards the balcony, I froze. It was Tracy. I could see that she was crying from thin silvery rings down her cheeks. The cold wind blew her dazzling white pyjamas and bit hard into her bare hands and legs, which she did not seem to realise. She stood on the same spot for a long time looking towards the capital; she was even not aware of what she was doing. She stretched her hand and touched the lowest barbed wire at the top of the wall fence, then brought her hand down hard on it. I moved away from the cantilevers. The barbs tore her soft palm and she looked at the fast flowing blood in the light of the moon. She rubbed the hand on her white pyjamas and made big red marks on them. She looked at her hand again and prickled it several times on the barbs until she leaned on the wall in pain. The three-legged cat crossed from the maintenance store in a high speed and climbed the wall like a lizard. I swore I was going to kill that devilish creature as soon as I could get my hands on it. I was convinced that it had a strong association with bad situations and was always the final signature to an unusual happening.

She attracted a security man who was walking around unaware of what was happening. He moved closer and talked to her but I could see that she was not responding. I wanted to walk down their but something kept me strongly rooted where I stood. The security man led her away in the direction of the college hospital. I was a complete failure in getting an answer to the puzzle of a girl who knew how to solve her own issues with bright reasoning. I did not think there was something that could have been bigger than the worst time in her life, which she had successfully come out of. I had come to have a lot of respect for her, which she did not know. I needed to tell Tracy one of those days that I respected her. For the first time, I felt stone hearted and rigid. I needed to think about people around me not when extracting information from them as a journalist, but as a human being who not only understood people's emotions but also respected them as well. Not because I was Brooks but because I was human. Was Tracy trying to commit suicide? I did not know. It was always difficult to know what went on in people's minds.

The clothes of the girl on the next block were swaying on the balcony as if they were fanning the sleeping people and pestering them to wake up early after a night of disturbance by their owner. She had gone to her room and accepted peace within herself when the same people she had spent the night keeping awake did not need the sleep anymore. They were not asleep at that time but lying on beds with active minds which had started performing endless calculations on the best thing they would do during the day to support life. As usual, they ended up with great ideas which carried few facts because they would be seen during the day selling sweets in the streets with a mind of owning candy shops and thereafter start something even bigger and walk out of poverty. They soon realised with a rude experience that what they were thinking was economically impossible. The night owl returned with a mighty flight like a war plane from the east and circled its tree to make sure it was secure before perching on it. It looked towards the horizon as if to approximate the time and then hooted four times. The roosters followed it with batting wings and crowing. Soon the morning would be filled with activity from people who got out of their beds because of mandatory reasons.

When I entered the room, Meyer was fast asleep with a pillow in his hands like a child while a movie playing on the screen had long ended without his knowledge. It was one of his peaceful days when he wanted to be on his own. I switched it off then covered him with a bed sheet before I pushed the curtain away and entered my room. I forgot to close the window the previous night and the mosquitoes, which had streamed inside on the hope that they would suck me dead, were nursing frustrations on the walls. They looked like sticky black crystals sprayed on the walls. I lit the mosquito repellant, which would have only managed to scare them away for few hours. They then would come again in numbers fatter and cleverer. That would have given me time to lock them outside. I used to buy such from supermarkets because they were more reliable sources. The street vendors and dubious dealers along Thika Road sold perfumed water which doubled reproduction and multiplication rates in order to maintain markets for the products. There was always an economical reason behind everything which happened along the road.

The standardisation of consumer products was taking a worrying trend. The economy was bad and people became creative in momentarily sustainable ways, which came to haunt them afterwards. One needed a constant update on what was happening along Thika Road to stay on the safe side. The previous week one of our students had bought the casing of an expensive cell phone full of mud inside, thinking it was a cell phone, and realised once the street dealer had disappeared. The dealer had expertly changed the sterile thing with an original phone after the deal. It was the same way fake money circulated among unsuspecting residents whose origin was difficult to trace. With advanced technology one could tell very little between original and fake currency. It made people rich within no time and they rose from mosquitoes and frogs to bungalows and handsome bank accounts. The people who acquired genuine richness were as few as insects in a stronghold of insect eating birds.

People rose in a way which would never be explained by an economic theory. But as they said, "money is everything." Anyone who did something dubious and it worked in his favour would have always done things in dubious ways and revise it only when it produced disastrous results. He would then change it. Not to the right way either, but to a different dubious direction. That was what was called 'dying by the gun.' Their minds did not seem to shift from the initial way which introduced them to property and money. Money acquired from fake currency business and drug trafficking was used to speed up buildings in attempts to grab tenants and investors, which would never be heard of unless they collapsed, killing people. Then it would emerge that they never met a single building requirement. The people they killed did not matter but the incurred losses did. There was a man, whose building had collapsed killing twelve people and he walked on the rubble with his hands on his head crying aloud for his lost investment.

There were times when the rich cried. Much as it was thought that the poor cried most of the time, there were times when they laughed too; like the rich. There was nothing noisier than a poor man who managed to jingle a few coins in his pocket. Such was the case with the toothless man who sold a baby donkey in the slums behind Mark's. Children called him 'termite' because he used to tell them to dance like a termite whenever he was drunk. The only wealth he would have put forward, if asked to account for the sixty-something years since he became conversant with the earth, was his donkey, which was a multi-purpose servant of its master. He used to ride on it as if it was a horse when he did not feel like walking. He would then boast about how he did not need to fuel his living vehicle the same way the rich did to their dead vehicles. The children would then form a chorus mocking him that he sold his teeth to buy a toothbrush. One of the things poverty taught him was that there was no need to get annoyed with the children who were products of their own cause and possible tired faces in the streets who would have succeeded owning donkeys.

Having owned nothing other than his donkey, he slept in a donkey station which had been established by an Asian writer who had seen it important to extend human kindness to the least valued animals by providing free water and resting space. 'Termite' used to sleep there on excuse that he was afraid someone might steal his donkey at night. Other donkeys were used to him as well. They never released kicks whenever he was around. He talked to them nicely in a donkey language and they heard him. One day his donkey mated with another while he was still asleep and it gave birth to a young one. He then sold it after two months for sixty shillings and he flew high like a millionaire the day he was paid. He would be heard shouting from the back of his donkey across the road when he was drunk that he would kill anybody and pay for the damages. To him it was a moment in his life when he had also gained voice. When the money was gone, he went silent and longed for another glorious time when he would sell a baby donkey again.

There were no silent people like those who should have shouted loudest, much as there were no busy people like those who had nothing to do. It passed unnoticed, except by those who were doing the same thing. It was a way of cheating reality and they claimed to get with from it. It gave them purpose just for that moment but within a short time they were back where they had begun. Their problems punished them by becoming bigger. They solved them by making wars within themselves, then spread them to others. Their families broke up and the lives of their children were not far away from those they had led. The same people behaved insanc to avoid questions of accounting for their lives. They became prisoners of liquor so that they would blame everything on it. They faked drunkenness so that they could stay dirty, because they had options of buying soap and staying hungry or eating and staying dirty. They would do anything except accept their failures and would talk anywhere except in front of important people. Yes, there were people who knew positive ways of using problems as bridges and utilising their time. They were people who rose from poor backgrounds but never allowed their families to struggle like they did. They were people who would talk before any audience and still be listened to.

Meyer's love-girl, Eve, did not understand that. She was a representative of people who knew how to fall in love but not how to get out of it. She would exploit her instincts but not her brain and be courageous in losing but a coward in thinking. She did not know the difference between appearance and reality. She made herself available for people like Meyer who did not mind dropping her to a basket of victims in a selfish art which degraded those who were said to be his, and they blindly thought it a promotion because imagining they had been used was something difficult to accept. They were products of their own deceptions and mirrored themselves helplessly like a pawpaw fruit being eaten by a fruit bird which had spent time eating guavas, pears and mangoes. Because they became too lazy to plug a hole sure like death, they would build a wall somewhere on the way. The youngsters after them followed suit because they thought it was the way everyone thought it should have been done and not the way it was supposed to be done, then the cycle would begin again.

When Eve refused to take my hand in front of Meyer's friends, I did not feel different. I was not surprised but perhaps what she should have known was that I did not spend nights longing for it. She did not understand and I was not trying to make her know that either. For something good, I had told her about the dangers of what she was doing. For something better I kept quiet. When she collected the items I shared with Meyer and threw them on my bed while I was away, I felt then she had crossed the line. I would have preferred not to say anything but I decided to remind her that first, I was not her age mate, and second, I was not her playmate. I would have also added that she was a child of darkness but left it at that. Poor parenting and those in her life incited her reasoning like a drum which was said to be played for a rabbit eating kales on the farm. She was a ripe fruit of the teachings like those of Bishop Paul Lennox who had congratulated an unmarried college girl for giving birth to a baby boy the previous week. He called the child a gift and congratulated the father too.

Someone like Bishop Lennox could misguide people, while others could refuse to be guided, like Eve. Those were some of the variations which brought about life or death. They were the only two things in nature which were never known to have intermediates. Some people along Thika Road knew where they belonged while others did not know. The true faces of that visible fact would be seen in the evening after work. Some would be happy to go back home while others went there because they did not have anywhere else to go. There were those walking with the arms of their dirty overalls tied around their waists. They were tired with their lives but would not commit suicide because they had no courage for it. They hated those travelling using automobiles but could not do anything about it. As a result they were hurt and in low spirits and the only way it would be seen was through growing thin every day and wearing desperate faces of hopelessness from which protruded eyes of hatred.

The people would blame something for their status and wish they were different. Those across the road would see those in college as privileged. They could never go because of reasons of money and background which denied them similar chances. In college, people suffered from relationships which did not work and guilt of expectations which sent them seeking refuge in pleasures that left their admirers confused. They would drink and have sex at their own pleasure and say they had reached where they wanted. Children and teenagers would think it was the way intelligent people behaved and jumped into experiments which crashed like a giant plane in the sea. The unlearned people would blame the learned who claimed they were being underrated as they pointed fingers at each other. Role models vanished like dew in the morning sunlight. It became a tricky thing to tell children to follow the steps of a successful person but avoid some of the things they did. The children decided to copy the wrong way because it was the easiest and the community portrayed them as bad examples once they perished.

I had stayed long in the village and in town. I had known college life inside out having successfully graduated from the school of journalism and then in a college of foreign sciences. I had seen and heard a lot as an investigative journalist. I did not need anyone to tell me that I understood many things, but I was also aware that many new things, yet to be understood, happened each day. That was nature, and nature was never to be fully understood. I saw men and women make bonds and I saw them separate. I saw people make lives and I saw others destroy them. There were many victims and victors just like there were heroes and villains. Adding one and the other from east to the west models like Tracy were rare. Her manual was her brain and she never did something everyone did. She was hard-working with undying determination and it never let her down. She excelled in most things and would think of new ideas each time.

Chapter Ten

The Gear for a Tear responded to my proposal in a long letter which said they would come to take a survey in a month's time. Haamid assured me that there would be no problem once they were interested, as long as they verified what was written in the proposal. They would then take feedback after which, if positive, the process of funding and establishment would follow. It looked like the dream I thought would take the rest of my life was not very far away and I considered myself lucky then. On one weekend I took some time off and visited the place in the company of Haamid and Tracy to make sure everything was okay. I found the land being utilised by locals for their own uses. There were animal tethers and cow dung all over the field and someone had cut down the trees at the hedges and used them to burn charcoal some few metres away. Disrespect for private property was an occupation in that place for people who did not have the vaguest idea of a legal process. There was that tendency of people thinking a person's property was idle because it had no use. They did anything they felt like, from keeping animals on their land and eating fruits from the trees, saying their children never ate them because they were always full.

The escalator to the floor of a good life was the joy of knowledge. Education was the key and its love was reciprocal. It took people places and rewarded them with privileges replacing hopelessness with blossomed ideas and the guesswork of darkness with the light that lit their entire lives. The limitations of knowledge and thinking faded with education and instead opened doors of imagination which brought with it discovery and innovation. Recognition and great success without education was as impossible as trying to lick one's elbow. The modern world did not allow seeing otherwise because the rise and fall of demand and supply in anything called for vital information in almost everything. The perception of even simple jobs in the past was fast changing. I saw some people become surprised when they were asked for certificates in the capital to be allocated jobs that needed simple skills like floor cleaning. It was education which had enabled me to acquire property at such a young age. Without it, I would not have met Haamid or learnt about the Gear for a Tear which had given me great hope in what I wanted to achieve.

I got myself into trouble during one of the community outreach programmes when I started telling the youth that if they wanted to be leaders of the country, they not only needed to be educated but also behave like they did. I saw part of the audience put an equal sign between me and an idiot. I did not know then that I was speaking to a mixed audience where a majority of them had dropped out of school years back. One of the main objectives which stuck in my mind whenever I was talking to young people was to incite them against illiteracy, ignorance, anxiety and excitement which more than often sent them rolling off track and then perishing in the sea of destruction. I did not have information then that I had touched the boils of resented lepers. The organisers made a terrible mistake by mixing them at the last minute without communication. Even when I was quick to adjust, I knew that the first impression had failed and part of that audience would not listen to what I was talking about.

There were several reasons as to why I wanted Tracy to see the site. Dedication to her dreams, which would have helped other people, was her first priority in life. Apart from the dream of a children's home she held onto, never to let go, she had survived the most dilapidated life in her childhood and understood the pain of suffering. Seeing what I had done would have lit her mind with possibilities and helped her feel closer to achievements even when they were imaginary or far in her mind. She was the only girl I knew who had great ideas, not only about what life was but also what it meant. It was not a difficult thing to know what kind of a person she was. Even when other girls rushed to beauty and fashion the moment they grabbed a magazine, she stuck on humanitarian titles and business. She was always updated on what was happening around the world and head statistics on calamities which affected people in great definitions. Constructive ladies spent time with news and documentaries while destructive ones spent time with soaps and fashion. That was why they were always fighting for remotes in television rooms.

I was enjoying the best moments in my youth at a time when the word 'leader' meant something different whenever it was mentioned. People frowned and clicked in chorus before rubbishing whatever had been spoken. That was because it reminded them of failed responsibilities and daily suffering. The leaders were seen as processing units of corruption and malpractices in the country which sailed high in the world whenever the word corruption was mentioned. They were the answers to the missing billions and reasons for stagnated development and reconstructive efforts. They slept with our mothers and daughters while we were watching and sat on state resources. They were the same people who killed our dreams with our eyes open and replaced smiles on our faces with anger and hopelessness. Surprisingly they would be re-elected back to the same positions the next time and would stay in similar positions as long as they wanted, demoting the people to stepping stones and reasons as to why they were always up there.

Offices, businesses, hospitals and morgues were institutions of corruption and tribalism. It was the same old tree with flowers of nepotism and roots of impunity which was so common that people used to forget it was the right direction. Paying illegal fees for services stretched from birthdays when safer delivery was required and all the life where survival was needed, then after death to speed up burial permits. Few individuals made life difficult for the majority, making daily activities a jungle which had rules of either eating or getting eaten. There were no smiles on faces until someone identified himself by the tribe, or better still, showed what he carried in his pockets. My father was a tribal discriminator who associated various evils to different tribes. He used to talk about 'our people' whenever he was referring to his tribe. One evening when we were watching television and four of the five prizes won went to one tribe in a cell phone competition, he said they should have called it the name of their tribe.

Good news of the new constitution brought blossoming hopes like flowers in spring. It was a great moment of the nation and desperate people who were dying to see change. At the same time other challenges were waiting like the fight against illiteracy. One day, I asked my stepmother what she understood about a constitution, and after thinking, she said it was a document of the government. When I asked her what the government was, she said it was a group of executives in Nairobi. For people like my stepmother lying to them was as easy as knowing what to do when one was hungry. Lack of information as to where the world was heading exposed people to anything. Having conducted several interviews, I understood that here were people who were exposed like grasshoppers on a plain surface below insect-eating birds. That was why Africa kept on switching off its light and stumbled upon death in the darkness. Whenever death and life met in darkness, life was likely to lose. Those who prayed for doom called the beautiful black continent a dark continent of apes and wild animals.

A lot of days passed since the time I first set my foot at Mark's. It looked like many centuries before and I had learnt many things too. I saw people make wars and peace. People break up and reconcile. I did not know what I thought of the students when I came, but at that time, they were like any other human beings who were bound to mistakes and excellence. They would shout out of carelessness and excitement but keep quite when they were done. They would travel near and far, but the stopping point was Mark's, which existed on general service. The institution was there always getting better each day and looking new with refurbishment but it added one year after the other as if they were blessings of value. Those who existed in it always felt new and special. Their days sped up the way they never expected because they always pleased themselves. That was the difference between me and them. The giant Thika Road existed in defiance, always standing in command, carrying vehicles and people to different destinations. Some were born on it while others died on it. Some from different causes while others by its own decision.

I had submitted the sixteenth edition of my investigative work since I entered Mark's, which made my television employers nod their heads whenever they saw me. The work had been tedious, but its recognition kept me yearning to do more; even when I knew that I did not need appreciation to do it. It was just my career and I loved it. I was willing to take a break and gather my wandering conscience after many nights on the balcony where the night owl was sure of getting me early in the morning when it came back. If it could have spoken, then it would have told me to take care of its tree while it was away. Even the three-legged cat avoided the rubbish bin at the far end of the corridor because it did not want to risk losing another leg. The animal had an extra sense for danger and lack of the fourth leg was compensated for by the sharpness of its brain. I wanted to gain a mind and the easiest way I would have done that was by emptying the mind which had accumulated an overflowing sequence of happenings. Even when I stood looking outside the window that evening, I was not trying to learn anything; I was enjoying everything that was down there by seeing no evil.

Someone knocked on the door and I went to open it. Meyer was away attending to his lessons and his several concubines knocked only when he was inside. I hardly saw someone come to see him if he was away from the room except his love-girl Eve. When I opened the door I found Eve standing there. I wanted to turn and go back to my room but changed my mind when I saw pleading and fear on her face. She was not the defiant girl who stared into my eyes months back when she wanted me to know that there were times when decisions were decisions. Her eyes were red and tired and her beautiful rounded looks had faded with stress and desperation. I closed the door behind me and led her to the playground when I realised that there was something she wanted to tell me. There were no players on sight after a day of strong sunlight and although it had died down, nobody wanted to play. When we were deep in the field she folded her arms and the self-confidence which had been built by respect for an emotion she mistook for self-esteem seemed to have left her overnight.

"I know that it is stupid of me to call you like this, more so after the things I said, but now I know I should have listened to you," she started.

I stood still and waited. I could see that she had weakened herself through crying and only the pain and change which looked permanent flocked her mind, bringing out weakness as the only external explanation.

"I have not come to waste your time."

"You are not wasting my time," I cut in.

"You do not understand," she said with quivering lips.

"Perhaps the best thing to do when a person tells you something is to listen and maybe something better is to think about it. Those are the things I did not do from the time you warned me about my relationship." Her full school uniform always reminded me that she was young. She was still in the delicate stage of a personal roundabout, which sent teenagers in several different directions.

"I visited a testing centre yesterday and tested positive," she said in confession.

"Meyer has done me an inhumanity, Brooks." She looked away.

It occurred to me in disbelief that what I had feared had happened. The three-legged cat yelled near the wall fence as it challenged a dog which was trying to rob it of a chicken bone. I was scared beyond words as memories of Rusell's mother came to my mind. She had suffered and died almost at the same age. I had seen it come like the gathering of clouds before a storm and tried to send a warning signal but it became too late. For the past few days Meyer had not gone to class and looked mentally disoriented. He spent his time in the room swallowing sleeping pills and antacids and seemed to have reached the final conclusion of what he wanted to do with his life. Even when Eve said that she had not told him about her status, I doubted whether he did not have information. My mind went to the day when I saw him through the window, as he lit medical prescriptions in the far end of the corridor and made sure they burnt to ashes before he moved away. Was it that Meyer had deliberately killed the girl?

A devil wind gathered from the parking to the east as she walked away. I was scared beyond words because I knew the implication of what she had told me. She was alone in one of the most difficult times, which changed her life forever. The people who had fanned her were nowhere to be seen then. They were the same people whose mind she had relied on and did everything because they did the same, but now she was lonely, nursing one of the biggest regrets in her tender life. What happened somewhere was always a sample of what happened everywhere and that was what I was thinking at that time. The wind gathered momentum and finally lifted a cloud of dust and loose materials from the ground. She lifted her legs into the coming cloud of dust like the tick of the clock on the wall in our room and the distance between us increased. The cloud of dust covered her and she walked into it without waiting for it to settle. When it finally settled she was gone. I never saw her again.

Ambassador Carlito personally invited me to his office soon after I had finished covering another story about the difference between people who work in the same environment. He had called me specifically to ask me if I could take an editorial job from a vacancy which had been created by the chief editor of the monthly newsletter. It was better paying than what they paid me where I was working then. I told him to give me time to think about it and I went away with a promise that I would talk to him soon. I did not want to quit my current job but there were various occupational dangers when working in places like the ones I did, things only a journalist would understand. After pondering it for a while, I decided that I needed a break and some space from turning my back every time there were steps walking behind me. Somewhere along life, it was good to accept change and given that the change that was beckoning was positive, I did not see enough reasons as to why I would have resisted it.

When I told the managing director that I wanted to quit, he was not happy. My articles had gained a lot of popularity and quitting at that time when our television was interesting and the newspaper was the best selling was too bad. I was sorry for him that I had decided to quit within such a short notice and regretted that they had to find someone else to replace me. He told me that if I needed salary increment then they would see what they were going to do about it but he did not know that it was not just about the salary. When I explained what had fuelled my desire to quit he understood and let me go. He was always good and took time to listen. He nodded his head, looking beyond his spectacles and understood that I was chasing dreams and was still to achieve them. He was thankful for the role I had played and appreciated all that time I had fed them great articles and special editions. The chief editor, who had been my friend for all that time, shed tears openly when he heard that I was going away but life had to go on.

Meyer the player's lifestyle did not change even after his life took off into another direction. Scores of unsuspecting girls still came to chew candy with him. What was annoying was that the girls were ignorant, as if they were born yesterday. What was more annoying was that I could not help them. The man ate as usual and watched movies throughout the night. His lesson attendance dropped and he changed from reading his notes to magazines and newspapers. I was torn between talking to him and maintaining silence because the urges in both cases were opposing like the song which split children into two groups when the rain was about to fall. One group would sing for the rain to come down so that they would slaughter an old donkey, while the other group would tell it to go away promising the same price. Things were never going to be the same again for the man who was living a life that many would have considered suicidal.

I called the student school telephone where my sister studied more often and we talked for a long time about life, especially about things which teenagers like her were prone to. I, as well, made sure I called home to speak to Rusell before the day ended. I needed to be at the Portuguese embassy for four hours a day and the commitment denied me the time I needed for my loved ones. Apart from my lessons, I needed to attend various Portuguese events and embassy meetings as the Portuguese club president and the chief editor of the weekly Portuguese embassy newsletter. I seemed to look at life from different perspectives each day. When I was young and growing I used to dream about making a lot of money and becoming rich but once I was comfortable I realised that there were times when people longed for different things, especially when they thought about the people they loved. I had money but it was not the money I wanted. I wanted an assurance that the people I cared for were always safe and sound, both mentally and physically. That was when I realized that I had been away from myself for such a long time.

When I started, I did not know anyone nor did anyone know me. But then I was a public figure who was known beyond the department because of the crucial roles I played at St. Mark's. It was the same publicity I had tried to dodge all that time but sometimes it was impossible to dine without clinking glasses. I did not know most of the people who greeted me along the corridors and college pavements. I had seen people ruin their lives and I had seen people make them. There were those who differed in the way they lived their lives, but in the end they made it, and that was enough reason to celebrate. Success was success in any way it was achieved and when people were in a celebratory mood, nobody was interested whether it was because of luck or on merit. The people were the same but the way they reasoned was what was different. What was important was that they were a large family who I referred to as my people. I was trying to become a man by doing what I wanted and what I was expected to do. I was glad as well that at long last I had set up a strong base in my hierarchy of needs.

There were two things which I had come to associate myself with whenever I was around Mark's. One was making a difference and feeling nothing. The second was getting commended about my long and handsome hair, and then say something to imply it was nothing. I remembered the first day when Mrs. Fabiano thought I looked weird with a woman tattooed on my arms. She did not know that they were paintings of my mother, who left us when we needed her most, and my younger sister, who was a little lovely thing. The flowers which were all over my arms always reminded me about their love. My mother loved flowers and she used to admire her second-hand dresses with big flowers which she bought down at the local market. She had a lot of bright species which she planted down in the flower garden, but it ceased to exist when she died. My sister seemed to take after her because she was always fascinated by bunches of flowers when we sat watching television programmes.

One evening I set time aside from work to walk around and see what the students were doing. It was difficult to know the details of every place in the enormous learning institution. Students only knew the places they frequented like lecture halls and their departments. The same faces that looked young and bright on the day of registration now looked hard and older. Others were bitter with swollen cheeks. They were faces of regret and resignation which longed for the time they would get out of there. The excitement and love that existed during the first days in college was long gone. That was because things failed to go according to their expectations. It was the simplest way of telling the difference between new and old students. They were full of frustrations and confusion. They were the same who said love was blind when they came and allowed themselves to fall freely into the traps of those who claimed they did not have a love like theirs before. They did not give them guarantee that they would not have a love more than theirs in the future.

The results of frustrated expectations were all over their faces. Girls had dumped their relationships in favour of expensive dates in the nearby city centre, moving up and down with anyone as long as they had money; towards the end they realised they were alone. They were more cautious, which did not help them much because they had wasted their time, and time had shifted roles to waste them. It was something which hurt them badly to think they had been used.

As a result of desperation they were willing to negotiate and started remembering those who were in their lives before, but as it happened, irreversible changes had happened beyond interference. When they realised they were functions with expiry dates on their faces, they did not know what to do other than become bitter with themselves and then to other people. War always started within oneself before it spread to others. They would be heard saying things to the effect that they did not want to get married or all men were beasts, to justify that they had been done an injustice.

There was a big difference between girls and boys when it came to falling victim in relationships. Boys were not in a hurry for anything and they knew even when they graduated they would start working and still come back and marry from the college. While to girls, it was a race against time. They understood that if they got out of college there was a likelihood that the boys they were likely to meet there at a later time would have been younger and that was why they looked for relationships as if they were working on deadlines. In the process they were reshuffled and used like cards of a game. There was nothing I knew that was more dangerous than a girl in a relationship towards the end of fourth year. That was because she focused on her life after college, and marriage was the only thing that was ringing in her head; therefore, she did everything it took to achieve the final results. It would even get worse when they were in constant pressure from home to bring forward a man who had proposed. To the boys it was different. They looked for reasons to breakup after the four years, with intentions of skipping suggestions of getting married.

As I walked towards the resource centre I passed a group of girls of who one was very pregnant, swinging her belly like a duck in the drizzle. What was interesting was that she was the one who was talking the loudest. The father of the expected baby was nowhere to be seen. She was among the few who decided to keep the pregnancy or probably got tired of terminating them. She was among those who had lost their youthful looks and needed to convince someone why their looks distanced themselves from their ages in order to be trusted. They were looks that easily told someone observant that she was one of those who had been used after hovering up and down restaurants and casinos with 'play boys' and strangers who had a large influence of money. Their time was well spent in alcohol and drugs and their trends were those of waking up and finding themselves sleeping with strangers. While I spent time studying lives in college, one day I told teenage girls in high school that passing examinations in college did not mean that the people there did everything right. It did not define intelligence in anyway either. I told them to think about examples of girls who passed highly in the previous stages and had joined college but were in homes taking care of babies singlehandedly, and I saw that they knew what I was talking about.

We were warming up for the great day when we were supposed to fly across the continent to Brazil, and it was impossible not to feel happy and excited. The class was unified for the common purpose then, and our friendship strengthened, given that we were close to finishing the race, which had started on rough road. We lost seven students who dropped out while two of them died from natural causes. When the material day neared I went with Tracy for a walk because we were free after the department postponed all lessons until the function was over. I used the time to tell her about life and its challenges and the best way I knew how to overcome them. She made me feel I was like her brother. I had no doubt that she was an intelligent girl, but I wanted to remind her to make sure she did not fall to any slip-ups. She was a good listener and always took her time, especially when I was talking to her. I was in particular concerned about her future prospects and how she intended to be of service to others who were less fortunate in the society. I also told her about 'the insect' but was careful not to mention Meyer or his love-girl.

I arranged on how work was going to be done before I took a leave from the embassy and we all boarded a plane to the capital Rio de Janeiro. There were vital signs showing that the common purpose that caused us to meet at Mark's was coming to an end. The unfamiliarity and pretence which had existed over the years faded away and there were more free talks and greetings. It was an implication that we were going to miss each other, especially after overcoming the test of time. We had developed fondness amongst ourselves without realising it, and even the worst characters hated in class were treated with kindness then as we fared on as one large Portuguese language family. Someone started a song from behind and others joined in clapping. I sang it too because I might not have had any other chance to sing with that big group who had gone down in history as a success. The last time we were singing like that was when we were going to play sports in a neighbouring campus. We repeated the same over and over, but it did not lose its taste.

We arrived in Rio de Janeiro, that great city known as *cidade maravilhosa* with people of different ethnicities and colour, yet all were hospitable. They say it's good to be home but for a time it was also nice to be away from home. It was a city of love and a reference point when talking about history and business. It was an ocean of love and a mile of greatness. Everything was defined and lovely because of the people with a great personality who were always smiling when giving directions. It felt nice, just like the soaps they acted there, which was one of their finest exports. People on holiday and merry makers from all over the world gathered to spend time and money there. Brazilian Portuguese was the order of the day there whenever communication was called for, and a little Spanish would do too. The sun rose from miles away and left bright orange skies when setting, which lit the waters below where the reflection looked like it always went to sleep under the waters. The people liked it, and we liked it too when we went around speaking their language as if we belonged there.

Even when they said 'home sweet home,' some memories took me back to my home country when I saw street children. Everything had its own reference and the reference was never a random selection. That was why best memories just happened good or bad. It was a community of street children I had seen in the capital and all around the slums which became hostile whenever its anger was triggered by hunger and insecurity. In one of my editions, which covered what it was like living in the streets, I spent four days and nights observing what they did from one place to another. After comments started flowing in from various civil rights groups and humanitarian organizations, there was a philosophical doctor who said I had gathered the video according to my own interests. I would have told him to reserve his comments for his dogs, but we were never allowed to exchange personal comments on an issue which had been released to the public unless under very special circumstances.

Mrs. Fabiano accepted Tracy's request that we visit the slums, which were popularly known as *favelas*, and children homes around the towns of Rio and São Paulo. I saw the agony and misery of people living in *Grota do surucucu,* that was one of the favelas in Niterói, quite close to the heaven of Rio where people came from far and near to spend and enjoy. They were not different from the daily lives we used to see in Kibera and Mathare slums. They were optimistic like any other slum I ever studied in the world, that one day they were going to make it and join the rest of the world in what they believed was softer life, then maybe abandon using drugs, which they claimed helped them stay blind about what was happening in their lives. They were people who believed their lives had not begun. Religious people often quote from the Bible that man shall not live on bread alone, but in that part of the world they did not live on bread at all.

Tracy openly shed tears when we visited various children's homes. She had a special feeling for children and other people, difficult to explain or compare. What affected other people affected her. Within a few minutes after we arrived she made friends with children and needed a lot of persuasion to convince her to board the trip vehicle. As if it was meant to be reciprocal the children were unhappy when she left. They would wave until the bus disappeared and then it would give her time to pull herself together again. Life might have been a journey but it would have been better if that became literal. I knew that there were several people who hated field work, but at the same time, seeing was believing. I was so satisfied with my own feeling at that time that I loved going to fieldwork. When everyone's face suggested that it was a good thing to be away from classes, and if all of us were wrong then I guess the group of wrong feelings made the whole thing a right. For the first time I felt I hated my room back in college together with its window which opened to the tree with the hooting owl and the favourite wall of the screaming three-legged cat.

The third day of the trip found us looking down at the great Amazon, which previously existed in my mind only in the books of world geography. The largest tropical rain forest on earth was beyond the description of life itself. It looked like a kingdom with an invisible king who was served by the components of climate, enabling him to nourish the vast stretch with endless cycles of rain, whose beauty was the thick green trees inside where existed thousands of animal and bird species. It was impossible not to feel natural away from cities and roads which tended to hide a lie about the cause of human existence. It stood gigantically with a description beyond words, and the untold truth was that it had a perfect definition of the distance between life and death through rivers and endless tributaries surrounded by prey and predator animals. The secrets of survival seemed to come behind the thick morning fog in the cool sunlight which sent warmth and freshness to as far as Rio de Janeiro and even beyond. It was difficult to get with such a lovely sight. It stood to explain the true source of love and happiness

Tracy stood looking at River Amazonia. It was difficult to tell the exact position it started and where it ended. Her arms were crossed and her eyes not blinking in concentration as she gazed to the distance up to where it disappeared inside the trees like Thika Road in a rugged landscape from the capital. The difference between it and the polluted rivers in Nairobi was its look of purity which was seen through the clear water reflecting the blue colour of the sky. Everything looked beautiful, even the coloured frogs which kept on jumping from the broad leaves to the water. They were different from the grey and yellow toads of Thika road, which appeared in a slight drizzle to mate and multiply as if rain was food. I did not care brushing though the leaves of chameleons, which differed from earlier days when I was a real coward and it sent me yelling like tethered goat looking at an approaching storm. I was slightly changing with time too and I then guessed that I was growing up.

Life itself was as long as the stretch of River Amazonia and the little things that gave it purpose of existence were like the tributaries and streams that constantly fed the river day and night. Like in life, it was through those mutual benefits that the river managed to regulate the water cycle, which was vital for the existence of life in that forest. If the rivers dried then every form of life in that place would have followed suit, and, like in human life, the existence and look of lives which would come after depended on that which existed before. As long as the river existed without interference, the little birds diving inside on the surface of the water would drink or wash with as much water as they wanted and the roots of the trees would suck several tanks each day, but the river would always exist.

Chapter eleven

There was a two month holiday vacation after the successful trip to Brazil. I went to see Meyer who was hospitalised due to immune deficiency complications. He looked beaten but was still defiant. Meyer was the same person even after his life took a rugged trend. He was still a great orator and would talk about life upside down as usual then repeat that the world was crazy and needed twice as many crazy people. He paused a little when he spoke about the people while staring at the ceiling then repeated several times how he hated them. The drip above his bed made him look weaker, not in his looks but in his voice. He had the gift of a wonderful body which was handsome all the time and against all odds, even in his condition; his doctor also seemed surprised. The man who had spent his better days with a flock of girls around him was then alone in a hospital bed wearing a numbered patient uniform and there was no likelihood that he would go back to his famous suits anytime soon.

"How are doing?" I asked him.

"What do you think?" he rudely replied with a question.

"I think you are going to be okay soon,." I said trying to sound polite.

"I see. Keep thinking." He coughed and turned to look at me with red eyes.

"I don't know why you people interest yourself with these stupid little things."

A nurse came and gave him some tabs to swallow. He put them in his mouth and fixed his eyes on the door. She stood there in panic with a glass of water waiting for him to take it and wash them down his stomach. When he did not take the glass, she told him that he needed the water. He said in a low scary tone that he had swallowed them. I was surprised just like her because he did not make a single movement in his throat. The nurse put the glass of water on the table and went away. When the door shut itself, he pulled a rubbish bin from the side of his bed and spat the tablets inside. There were crying children from the wards from needles which were inserted into their soft flesh and their mothers comforting them by promising them gifts to stop crying. I did not know what else to say or how to say it.

"It has been a pleasure at Mark's," I said.

"Yes it has been," he said.

"You know you are my roommate, man." "Oh, I didn't know. I thought your roommates were ghosts and night birds on the balcony."

It was becoming cold. I covered his legs with a duvet and sat back on my chair. I wanted to tell him that he was an important person to me and that I loved him, but I saw it difficult judging from his dejected mood.

"There are times and season for everything," he started.

I listened without interrupting him.

"That's what your Sunday school teachers did not tell you. So you can agree me that you used to go there for nothing. Mark's lies and the same applies to you. They call it a higher learning institution? Have you ever asked yourself 'about what?' or 'for what?' Do not answer me. Go and tell Mrs. Fabiano to start awarding drug abusers and prostitutes, like Irene as well. You are her favourite and she will listen to you, maybe."

He paused and cleared his throat.

"There is a time to be born and a time to die. You know there is one thing I have never paused to think about you, Mr. Ishimwe."

It was the first time he had used my second name.

"What is it?"

"That you are a pretender and a hypocrite."

"Oh, really?"

"How does all that information you collect about the lives of people help you? I do not want your answer. You silently claim that you are real in the way you look at things huh? Let me tell you one thing though even when I'm sure you are not listening. There will always be people who behave differently from the streets of Nairobi to those of Manchester. If people behaved similarly, then maybe there would be no death or life."

He cleared his throat and added something.

"Another thing you should know is that you are not what they think you are."

"Who is 'they'?" I asked.

"Keep thinking. You call yourself an investigative journalist? Discover what happens around you, and when we meet in hell come for some cash."

I did not interrupt him because I was trying to make sense from what he was talking about.

"I heard you mumbling about the distance between life and death in your sleep one night when you were supposed to be dreaming about something constructive. Let me tell you about the distance you were talking about. The law of nature either keeps the distance or narrows it, depending on what they feel suits a situation. That is to say, they do not to consult you. The distance cannot be kept forever and understanding that is what is called reality. Not the way you define it unless you never read evolutionary books about natural selection."

I was convinced that Meyer was insane. I did not believe all those things came from his mouth. It then occurred to me that time had modified him to believe what he thought about his lifestyle. From the time we had our first talk I had dismissed his reasoning as immaturity and thought he would grow up to clear his inapplicable theories from his mind. If he talked like that even at that level then he had modified his life with a no turning back. After I interpreted all that within a matter of seconds I restrained myself from talking about anything which would have indicated giving advice or trying to cheer him up. I kept the talk casual and polite as much as I could.

"There was a man who had two coins and believed they possessed the luck of the day," he started.

"Each morning he used to toss them at the same time and if he got heads then he considered the day very lucky. If he got a tail and a head the luck was half but if he got only tails then his day had no luck at all. If the day had no luck at all it did not mean he had bad luck, and that is what I want you to know."

He broke into a long scary silence while he cleaned and scratched inside his ear with his small finger.

"The biggest of the times and seasons for everything is a time to be born and a time to die. Birth is just birth and death is just death."

He covered his head with the duvet.

"You know I love you, man," I said.

He uncovered his head and started laughing, increasing his voice gradually until the laughter was ear shattering. When I saw that he was not stopping, I rose up and walked out. The sound which left his mouth formed a series of echoes which spread to the room and beyond the adjacent wards. I walked faster to get out of that sickening place. When I was out of the hospital I felt like part of my life was gone.

Three weeks later he died. I felt depressed and empty, like a tree which had been robbed of all its branches and was not sure whether it would have any before it was cut down. After I received the sad news that day, I went with Russel to Uhuru Park and wished something frustrating would happen to me so that I would feel more terrible. Russel was then staying with me for his holiday and he was the only dearest thing close to me. I sent him away to play with packets of biscuits. He was a quick friend maker and within a short time he had friends all over him. I did not hear the vehicles along Uhuru highway hoot nor did I sense the smell of the contaminated air of their exhaust pipes. Very few things mattered to me at that time. I did not know what I thought about Nairobi or Rio then nor did I understand what real life meant after Meyer called me a layman the last time I saw him alive. I looked at Russel play in innocence. He would shout "Daddy! Daddy look!" He would repeat the same until I commented on what he was doing. He might not have known his real parents, but he was lucky that I made sure he did not miss anything. There were several others out there who had nobody to look at them or anywhere to go.

People along the highway were hurrying to different directions in well-defined parallel movements like ants in long paths. They would pass each other but never collided. Even vehicles followed the same trend and all were ants heading to underground tunnels of their houses and shanties to emerge again above the ground another time when opportunities presented themselves for the endless journey of life. Most of them did not create opportunities like few great individuals but rather waited for them and that was why they were always in the streets in great numbers. Someone would crash out of the path like Meyer or meet a predator along the path like Faith while others would be too weak to walk and pushed out of the path to die from the scorching sun or hunger, but there were always ants on the tracks. Always. The people were ants and the only difference was that what ants failed to achieve in sizes, they achieved in numbers.

I had lost my concentration in almost everything and everyone around me. It looked like Russel was the only person who existed in the whole world when I gazed with blurred vision beyond Kenyatta Conference Centre which stood proudly as the tallest building in the capital. All other voices did not exist except his, which sieved itself from those of the other children who were playing with him. I did not feel the city looked beautiful anymore, and I saw the buildings as just dead structures moulded out of blocks and metal before they were made compact by several bags of cement. They did not talk and they did not grow. They would not provide answers for several questions which kept on repeating themselves in my overflowing head. Russel came and jumped on my shoulders from behind. I told him to sit and sent the other children away.

"You know I love you, dad," he said.

It was the first time he had said that before I could even tell him what I wanted to say. I did not know that someone loved me and it was the loveliest thing someone could have told me at that time. While the whole world spat on my face, Russel was the only person who seemed to understand.

"I love you too, son," I replied putting my hand on his shoulder.

"Can I ask you something?"

"Sure. Go ahead."

"What is wrong? I do not like that look on your face," he said.

He turned to look at me as if to confirm what he had observed. I turned my face away. I knew it was not nice to look at. That was what I wished Russel would not have seen. I felt more ghostly than the sound of the screaming three-legged cat and weirder than the face of the hooting owl on the tree outside my window.

"Dad is fine," I said.

"When you will grow up like me only a few things will make sense to you."

"I understand," he said.

I knew he did. Russel was always fast to interpret what I said, and sometimes I wondered whether it mattered at all that I was not his biological father.

It was easy to accept that one shilling in the pocket never jingled when I looked at the social report card of my life. At the same time, more shillings were likely to turn chaotic and probably make a hole in the pocket which would have led to owning no shilling at all. However, it was a difficult thing for the shilling to save itself and its value never interested anyone. Times were fast changing and playing hero was the wrong approach. The people did not want to listen to any of that and they were always on the race to fill in their statistics of pride and heroism, which did not add anything to their lives. I was a single, lonely coin and that was why it was difficult for me to jingle. Other people spent time together like many coins and that was why they easily jingled. It was the reason their sounds were likely to attract expenditure from nature through group decisions of self-destruction and disastrous collective responsibilities in houses of entertainment and drugs of influence. Their flower petals were unending bodily desires and pleasures which ripened into fruits of regret and death. My problem, which was not their problem, was they never realised nor did they learn. They were not willing to.

I received an approval letter from The Gear for a Tear the day Meyer was going to be buried at the Lang'ata cemetery. I was torn between joy and sadness. The head of the Japanese department wanted me to speak at his funeral, but I refused completely. Haamid came to keep me company but still, the emptiness was there and he was like one little grain in an empty bucket. We kept on following each other without speaking, like small children. They said there was a time and season for everything and Meyer had said that there was time to be born and a time to die. Memories flashed through my head like they happened yesterday. He was the only person I knew when I first came to college. It did not matter anymore whether he was bad or good but what I knew was that we were going to miss him.

My lecturer Maria Fabiano called me for a talk in her office when the session opened. It was the first time we met after the successful academic trip. We were the first students geared for graduation in Portuguese language since the establishment of the college eight years earlier. She was determined to make a stunning excellence on what was going down in the college's history. She was calling and talking to people she thought were key players who she knew would have made that happen. I found her filing some data, and when she saw me she took a deep breath and smiled, welcoming me. I did not know that our talk was a little different from the one she held with the other students.

"How have you been?" she asked in Portuguese.

"I have been doing well Mrs. Fabiano," I replied.

"We are going for a walk," she said.

She closed a file she was looking at and then took me outside. I did not know what she wanted to tell me, but I knew that talking in the open while walking would make her exhaust whatever she wanted to say.

I was attentive and respectful as we walked towards the woods. She was a great person and most of the things I had achieved while I was studying at Mark's was because of her help, which either made me realise my potential or exposed me to several advantages.

"You are rarely available these days," she started.

"Has the work been tedious for you?"

"A little," I said.

"I have been moving up and down the embassy and lessons."

"I know," she said.

She cleared her throat and kept silent for close to a full minute.

"It has been a pleasure to have you as one of my students all these years I have been in this department."

"Thank you," I said.

Even when her voice sounded a little tough whenever she was talking about something important it remained the same that day. I knew she was aware that I did not take her for granted and I was not ready to let her down.

"You have been a role model to your fellow students and many people out there but it is not enough," she said.

"I want you to look over there," she motioned towards the end of the woods.

There were students sitting on the benches in pairs with their hands over each other's shoulders. They were whispering into each other's ears or eating snacks and looking towards the direction of the playing fields. They were flirting at a bad time and giving each other endless love promises. She kept on walking along the woods, pulling her overgrown hair away from her face.

"I want you to make those youngsters understand what they should do with their lives. It is not going to be easy but you have to do this as a priority wherever you are."

I did not know how I was going to make millions of people understand. She spoke in good faith, like any other good mother but what she was talking about was what had failed terribly for all the time I spent exposing what went on in darkness. I did not know how to tell her all that without looking like I was one of those people who quit. There were millions of ignorant youngsters just like the millions of activities they grouped themselves into. She was not aware of what I had seen for all the time I stayed at the balcony. She did not have any information about my late roommate, nor did she know about the hundreds of others who were following a fate similar to his.

"Doing good always will free you from guilt of selfishness about information that can be important to other people. Remember doing good is a virtue which does not have regrets."

I nodded my head to show that I understood.

"Just like the sun rises and sets as well as light alternates with darkness, doing good always will make other things come to pass but you will always remain. That is one fundamental thing I have learnt in the world."

After the brief talk with Mrs. Fabiano, I did not want to go back to my room because it was empty and lonely. After Meyer's belongings were taken to his home it looked even bigger, like a hall which would have held a small conference. It even formed an echo when someone was speaking inside there. I did not want at all to go and see Tracy, but it I did not know of any other person who was more accommodative and peaceful. I wanted to be in company that would not have told me anything about good and bad. There were times when company was very vital. A man from the village whose son was working in England went to visit him and see how he was faring on when he was given an invitation. When he reached there he started complaining and wanted to come back home as soon as possible. He said that he did not have enough time with his son like he did when they were back home. Far away from the hefty time he was used to idle back home, he found that everything went with squeezing in appointments here and there and the longest time he met him was for fifteen minutes because he was always needed at work.

A majority of the people in towns and country sides did not need appointments to see each other. That was because they were always available. There was a friend of mine whom I worked with who told me about what he observed when he visited an Asian country that had three times the population of our country. Despite the fact of the huge population the people would not be seen. One could have done a head count in the streets. Unlike the vast numbers who were seen walking up and down the roads going nowhere, those people were always in their places of work or doing something constructive. If one wanted to know that people were doing nothing, all he had to do was to walk down the roads and see how they confined themselves in specific places playing games the whole day. Even in the villages, they were always there at roadsides supporting their buttocks with walking sticks, talking about something that had happened in a distant village, probably about a person who had died. If something happened in the streets, like people fighting, the attracted crowds could have easily explained how people were idle.

I found Tracy preparing to get out for some air. I was glad because I did not want to confine myself in a room at that time. We had already started missing Mark's, which we had so much come to associate ourselves with when we talked about what we were doing. The new students who were warming up for the next intakes looked like small children who did not know anything about college. It was impossible not to feel older when one was a finisher even when some of the new students were older. The lower levels of the units we had registered years back felt like those people met when they first entered elementary school preparatories. Mark's did not know anything about that. It was always there to welcome and served anybody it gave a chance to study there. It was several months before finishing and we were springing for the final whistle which was the shortest and sweetest lap.

We walked into the play grounds which were full of activity at that time. Students were happy, shouting and playing which was a strong sign of friendship. It felt good to think like that. We kept on walking while looking at what they did until we were away in the trees towards the fence.

"You know life is a journey," she said smiling.

"Yes, it is," I agreed.

"Some travel with by air while others by road or even by water. It depends on destiny or what one wants."

She was a little philosophical that day.

"Accidents can happen along the way, you know. It is when it is realised that all the means of travelling are prone to accidents. If one is lucky then life goes on and it does not matter whether one was travelling by plane or bicycle."

I laughed because I did not think Tracy would ever use such things to explain her point.

"What are you laughing at?" she asked, a cheeky smile playing on her lips.

"Nothing," I said.

I could see the window of my hostel from that point. I could see that it was open and I had forgotten to close it when I went to attend the afternoon lessons. Two little birds were playing on the panes.

Tracy creased and then released the top of her face almost at the same time. With that simple action, the smile on her soft face disappeared. She crossed her arms and looked as far as the horizon where the surface of the earth lit the sky. The only thing that moved was her chest, which rose and fell as she pulled gulps of air one after the other. The numerous buildings towards the capital looked falsely swallowed inside the green trees, which were so few that it was seen from the distance. Signal boosters stood high up in the air and looked like they were just inches away from the blue sky, which was just an imaginary thing existing in books of literature and observation science. The numbers of people whether idle or busy would not be seen then because they were covered by the features of the landscape. I did not feel a stranger then, the way a journalist always feels when collecting information. There was something about that night but I did not know what it was.

She narrowed the distance of her imagination beyond the horizon to somewhere nearer by blinking her eyes and sniffling with the cold air. She tried to speak but failed. She tried again for the second time but only managed to open her mouth. She shook her head and what I saw next were tears rolling down her eyes. It saddened me to see Tracy cry.

"What's wrong?" I asked politely.

"There is something I wanted to tell you," she said turning her eyes away.

"Go ahead and tell me," I encouraged her.

"I can't," she said choking with tears.

She turned to look at the barbed wire above the wall fence and it reminded her of something. She looked at her hands but there was nothing on them. They were just tender and smooth months from the day I watched her from the window of my room prickle herself on the barbed wire until she drowned in pain and blood. Something was wrong. I held her shoulders and made her look at me in the eyes.

"I'm your best friend Tracy," I told her.

"Just tell me and I will understand. You always know that."

She looked at me trembling in fear and panic. I saw mercy for her. She shook her head.

"I can't," she repeated.

"Do you know that I hate seeing you cry?" I asked wiping her eyes with the back of my hand.

A flock of little migrating birds flew from the giant trees towards the setting sun. They lit the sky with beautiful patterns of flight altering them at regular intervals. Two pied crows kept on spoiling the flying pattern by dining in between, making them scatter before they regrouped again. There was no sunlight that evening and no strong winds either. She shook herself from my grip and broke free.

"I should have told you Brooks!" she shouted.

"I should have told you!" she repeated and ran away into the trees.

I let her go. What was Tracy regretting which she should have told me? I turned to go to my room but changed my mind and boarded a vehicle to the capital. The music in the passenger vehicle was loud but it was not loud, enough to erase what was going on in my head. The blue light inside and my blurred vision prevented me from seeing outside, but I was aware of the places I left behind as the vehicle sped in the evening, which was free of traffic police.

It had been five months at the balcony since the day Tracy failed to tell me what the problem was. She was in different and unpredictable moods and ceased to be the girl I always ran to whenever I wanted to speak to someone who would understand. With time she looked sick with depression and weakness; I affiliated it with the mental stress that sometimes sunk people into depression. I failed to find a way to help her. I had made a decision. I wanted to speak to Mrs. Fabiano about the whole issue so that she would attach her to the college psychologist who came occasionally, but I did not know how that was going to be possible because the final examinations were nearing. While I was torn between two opposing decisions she knocked on my door one evening and told me to join her for a walk in the playground. I hated going with someone to that playground for reasons I did not know. She had grown as thin as a praying mantis and her youthful looks were fast disappearing. I could not tell when she had last made her hair, which disagreed on top of her head. I wanted to make a last attempt to talk to her and I took time to frame my words as we descended the stairs.

"You have been my brother, Brooks," she started when we were a safe distance away from people.

"I'm always your brother," I said.

"I know that we have been having our differences lately but it will be a good thing to give my apology here while time permits."

"You do not need to because you will never offend me, Tracy," I said.

"Double tragedy happens and can happen in life, and if you can remember I never led something I can call a life but when I thought I was getting my life back it became unfortunate that was never going to happen."

"What are you driving at, Tracy?" My tension had reached breaking point.

"I made a simple mistake the first time I set foot in Mark's and it has turned out to be a big regret."

"What did you do?"

"I had a brief intimate encounter with Meyer."

"What?"

"I got excited. That was the mistake I made. So near can become so far. I had preserved myself to shape up my life and then fall in love with a man whom I would share the rest of my life and change perceptions of what I really thought about life."

I was not listening then and I felt my head was breaking. She continued talking as her words hit me like bombs striking stronghold targets.

"I was not a pecked fruit before I knew him. Not even unpeeled at a single time before I met him here at Mark's. He talked to me so nicely and politely looking at me with those humble eyes. I thought he was what I was looking for all my life, only to discover it was a lifelong terrible mistake."

"It's over, Brooks. No more stories about children's homes and no more talks about serving other people."

I let my cell phone fall free to the ground. Just then the three-legged cat yelled with all its strength as it was fighting with another cat near the wall fence. I left her there and headed to the hostel. I wanted to kill Meyer with my own two hands. I wanted to show him that someone could become a killer by starting with his first victim, and I wanted to start with him. When I could not walk fast enough I ran. I pushed aside a girl who was walking down the stairs and hurried up the room. When I opened pushed the door aside and entered, I looked for him but he was not in his room. The room stared at me empty and void, like a yolkless shell. I looked everywhere from his wardrobe to under the bed but he was not there. I knew he was somewhere looking at me. It then dawned on me like a flash of light in the darkness that he was lying dead in the cemetery. I did not believe he was dead because his ghost was all over haunting the living direct from his grave.

I left my room and headed to Lang'ata cemetery where Meyer sent shockwaves to as far as Mark's and beyond. I had a lot of questions I wanted to ask him. I always treated him like my friend but I did not know why he turned his anger on me. Anyone who laid hands on Tracy laid hands on me. It started raining when I was entering the cemetery. The drops hit the ground scattering the dust grains, slowly at first then fast as it increased. The drops wetted the ground and turned the dust particles into mud after which it paved a way to a surface runoff. My clothes were soaked in the heavy rains when I walked in between the rows of epitaphs reading the names until I found his. *Discover what happens around you.....*It was even beyond my imagination that Tracy would have allowed such a person near her. A guard looking at me from the distance did not interfere despite the fact that it was past time to be at the cemetery.

The rains fell heavily and my soaked clothes clung to my body. I shouted at him but he would not hear. I called him names and anything obscene which my mouth would empty but he did not respond. I asked him endless questions but he did not reply. Lightning flashed from the south in the darkness, splitting the sky in two with a blazing zigzag line. Thunder struck a tree with a vengeance to the east, shaking the ground in an ear-shattering blast. That was when I realised Meyer would not hear, no matter how much I shouted. I went down onto my knees and broke down like a child. The lights of the capital and beyond were as glittering as always. Those in the distance beyond were shining too, even when they were dimmed by the moisture of the precipitation. Suddenly, I heard Meyer's voice laughing at me in a mighty voice like thunder. The voice repeated itself in my ears as I walked out of the cemetery the same way it did when I went to see him in the hospital.

There was no passenger vehicle that could have accepted to carry me, after all, the sudden downpour had started and stopped on me. I paid for a taxi which took me to back to Mark's. I realised that it was difficult to avoid the college because it was part of me at that time and always. It was some hours before midnight when I staggered up the stairs to my room shivering like a butterfly in winter. Tracy was standing in the balcony with folded arms. When she saw me she came and held me tightly.

"You are my brother, Brooks," she said.

She turned her eyes towards the capital and then closed them. One by one the lights beyond the capital went off until the whole place was swallowed in darkness. Even with the darkness, life existed in those places, but above all there was the capital.

Chapter Twelve

t was four years and two days since Tracy died. I had worked for three months as the ambassador of Kenya in Portugal. I was in my home country for the official opening of the women and children's hospital as well as the children's home in the next compound, which I had initiated years ago with the help of Gear for a Tear. I named the hospital *Agostinho Women and Children's Hospital* in memory of the Portuguese father who dedicated his life to serving the less fortunate in the society. That was the only way he would have been remembered even in the generations to come. I called the children's home *Tracy and Faith Children'sHome* after the two girls who perished when their time was not due. Tracy might not have achieved what she wanted in her life but I had done it for her. I hoped that she would have smiled even in her death after the dedication she devoted the whole of her life to materialised under my supervision. As for Faith, she was the best thing that lived and one of my best teachers when I was still young. Her son Russel, who she left under my care, was not a commitment but a gift that shone light on my life.

The former Portuguese ambassador, Diogo Carlito, was present to witness the official opening ceremony. Haamid who was at the time working at the law firm was also present among other invited guests and officials from Gear for a Tear. My home village which was figuratively a bush a few years back was rather different at the time. It had not changed much but I could tell it was on the right path. Various artists from the country and my friends from overseas were performing, making the event look lively. When my time came, I gave a speech insisting on the importance of education and becoming useful to other people. I took the audience years back and reminded them about unfortunate people like Faith, the girl who was born like an angel but was buried like a dog, then revisited the life and dreams of Tracy, who most people did not know, even those who were with her at Mark's.

"The women can now give birth as much as they want," Haamid joked after the speeches were over.

I laughed.

"The children can have a place to pass the night too," I said.

"Sure," he agreed.

"You know life turns around, man," he said looking around.

"True," I said.

"Let me hope there will always be stories about Mark's even when we will grow beardless like Mahatma Gandhi," he said sniffling.

I laughed. Haamid looked like he always knew the secrets of happiness.

There was a distinguished guest that day who was silently walking around alone to see what people thought about what was happening and understanding them. It was my sister Eunice, who had then developed into a young beautiful youth. She was in her first year on campus. She was always imagining and looking for answers in what she thought were puzzles of life. When she saw that I was alone she advanced towards me.

"You know it really does not matter anymore whether we grew up without a mother when we were so young," she said.

"Our mother is alive because we are," she said smiling.

"And you, stupid thing, are my role model," she said slapping me on the cheek.

Even Russel who was laughing with his friends seemed to have developed internal happiness and peace. He had accepted in totality that I was his father, which was a nice thing to know.

"I was thinking about a having a family reunion," Eunice said.

"Okay. We can talk more about it."

"Sure. Do not worry. More cows have calved down at home and you can drink drums of milk to compensate for the two years of starvation you were given to teach you about manners."

My father was in high spirits that day. When he congratulated me I had all reasons to believe that he was saying it from the bottom of his heart. He was the same though. I had realised with time that my father did not know how to put some things into words. Anyone who did not know that would have easily misinterpreted him because what he spoke and what hc meant, were different things altogether. We were just a family of three after my stepmother went away on her own because she was barren and would not give birth to children. My father was a bad persuader and always let things to take their own cause. He let her go when she told him that there was no way she was going to stay in a family of children who did not belong to her and that she felt like a total stranger. Nevertheless if success had something to do it then we were bound to succeed.

Before I left the country I received a wedding invitation card from Irene, the 'bad girl' who was my neighbour back at Mark's. The last time I saw her was during the colourful graduation ceremony, at which I was awarded with first class honours. She was one of the few lucky ones who had withstood the test of time. I did not know how that happened, but nature was always something difficult to understand. That was because, despite the life she led, she graduated with a second class and began working with a foreign company. She sounded decided and I was interested to see what she looked like. It seemed like the end of cigarette puffs on the balcony and there were to be no more hooting owls on the tree or yelling cats along the walls. I agreed with Haamid in totality that life did turn around.

In some of the situations, a person would ask himself why a certain person did not die instead of another one. But as it happened, everything had a reason, and it was easy to understand but difficult to explain. Before I accepted that, every day I woke up holding a grudge against the world. That was the feeling which failed to leave me many days after Tracy painfully passed away. I did not understand and I did not want to. There was no reason why Tracy who made a single little mistake, was being punished heavily by the so-called nature, which she had trained herself to handle. I did not know why she left us when life was most promising and when thousands of homeless children were waiting for her, while merry makers like Irene were out there and were meant to last. That was the only thing that made me believe that luck existed. To me, Tracy was double tragedy, while to people like Irene, it was by chance which only religious theory would explain.

When Irene came to see me in the capital she was a different girl all together, just like I had predicted. She looked younger and more beautiful. Her eyes were not red for lack of sleep and even her style had changed.

She was grown-up and real because she did not talk a lot. Beside her was the man she intended to marry. As I shook their hands, I realised time had changed her forever and our relationship then was different from the one we had on the balcony at Mark's under the ageless, hooting owl. I welcomed them to their seats.

"I quit smoking," she said sitting.

"Congratulations," I told her.

We talked about what had happened for all that time since we parted from Mark's. She was one of the few people who had her life back and had accepted to live again. Life was about choices and Irene had certainly made a good choice for herself. Like my sister said during the official opening of my home village project: It did not matter anymore that we grew up without the love of a mother. It did not matter anymore that Irene did not lead a normal life when she was young. Two months later she walked down the aisle at a colourful wedding, which I attended.

Even when I considered myself grown up it did not mean I stopped thinking and learning from the things I saw either in the country or abroad. I spared some time away from duty and took walks around social places to see what people were doing. As usual, I learnt the same thing. People were ever changing to suit circumstances and time. Each and every day some of the values which existed in the past were less considered with time and options with more values worked well with the people. Learning went on and on all through life and the faster someone would learn the better chances he stood. That was the basic principle which supported life anywhere in the world.

There was a man who used to sell bread using a bicycle when I was still in college, and when I came back from abroad I found him still in the business.

The only difference was that he had new pedals for the bicycle. He had even perfected the style he used when boarding it. He pushed if forward before he jumped on top then sped down the slope with crates of bread on it. He would deliver the breads to retailers and then get empty crates in exchange. His bicycle was that of the old model and the only time I saw him bend over it was when he was pumping pressure into the tyres. I did not know where exactly he used to take his money because he usually counted a lot of cash before putting it in a deep pocket which he had sewn himself for that purpose. The pockets were reinforced with repetitive sewing until there was no way the money could have escaped from the pocket. The shopkeepers were used to what he was doing until they nicknamed him 'the miser bread winner.' He rejected the name when children started making fun of it, and he only responded when his customers called him by his name. He was one of the people who was satisfied with the little that he had.

A cow, which moos is the one given the calf. It was a common saying back in the village whenever they were distributing money for various projects after the self-help project I had helped them start while I was just a young journalist. The members borrowed the money and paid back with a profit and the cycle went on. It was amazing to see the potential of people whenever opportunities crossed their paths. I was one of the people who believed that even when I had injected a few thousands to initiate the process, the people would not have made it to those heights. They were a poor community with numerous dependents, but their reasoning was great and the rules they set amongst themselves were followed with strictness. They had managed to do farming and those who had farms previously had improved them for bigger productions. The hypocrisy and pretence which had existed sometimes back vanished, and they would talk more admirably about people who had made it to great heights. They had accepted the inevitable, which they decided to join after failing to beat.

I was aware of the fact that the world was always going around the same way people were changing. Desires and preferences changed too. For better or for worse that was the way it always was. When I was young and still growing I used to look at other people living in poverty and tell myself I did not want to lead that kind of life. It made me work tirelessly because I knew the only way a person would have achieved his dreams was by becoming stubborn with them and building a strong base in such a way that even the strongest waves would have not been able to sweep them away. It did not matter at all how one started a race. I looked at the number of people we started pursuing dreams with when we were still young and did not know much about the world. The difference between me and them was that I did not have someone who took my hand and made part of the paths I chose a gambling game. I did not do what all people did, but I did what I thought should have been done. When I finished the race I found that I was almost alone.

They say opportunities presented themselves, but then they rarely presented themselves towards my direction. When I looked how far I had come I realised that opportunities did not present themselves at all. I always looked for them and finding them was not an easy task. I was enjoying one of the prestigious positions in the society and sailing high in the world of fame and pride. I did not struggle whenever I wanted something because I had the power of money and huge experience at that time. I did not sleep hungry nor did I pass the night in the streets. I knew what it was like spending nights in the cold because I had done the same while I was preparing news for the *Worldreach* television. Even when I did not sleep hungry the fact that people slept hungry in different places was for real. There was a time when a group of executives decided to stay hungry when they were soliciting funds for hunger victims and almost all of them did not go beyond lunch time. By two o'clock they were yawning young ones of a bird.

Even when people yearned for different things at different ages, I was careful not to be misguided by desires. I had witnessed the way they altered choices and ruined lives. If they spared lives then they modified them in such a way that it became impossible to come back again. The rest of the days which remained were those of regrets and bitterness, if it did not cause misery. Bad decisions disabled the trends of life and that was what I wanted to avoid as long as I was alive. I personally had no regrets in the decisions I made and that was because what I did not achieve was because it was beyond my will. The best way I gauged the quality of my decision when things went wrong, was first to ask myself what kind of decision I had made earlier on and then ask myself what another person would have decided. When we used to compete in class, my secret weapon was the strong self-belief I had. If I prepared for an examination and there was a question I could not answer then nobody would have answered it. On countable occasions I saw someone get an answer right that I got wrong.

While I was enjoying the most prestigious position at my age, I realised that I needed to put what had passed behind me and move on. I met Adelina when I was in an official function in Brasilia, Brazil. We rarely communicated because of the commitment that my job called for. She was working as a management consultant after finishing her masters. We talked about the Portuguese event, which felt like it had happened ages before and laughed it off when I was then vying for the position of club president. Sometimes when someone was up the ladder it was difficult to imagine the kind of stones he stepped on to reach in his position. The position then looked so low and far away, and I don't think it was as difficult as it looked when we were doing interviews and wooing for votes. Some things were not as simple as they looked but they were very important when one needed to keep on climbing the ladder if he was not willing to come down.

We grew fond of each other because she was the only friend at the time that I got along with, even when we only met for one week while I was still studying at Mark's. When we fell in love, we decided to consult her mother and find out what she thought about it. One evening when I requested her to allow us get married she was stunned that at long last Adelina had decided to get married. Mrs. Fabiano was a person who always walked with decisions on her finger tips and when she told me that she wanted to meet us both, I knew that she was not going to look for something to say but it helped her compare her own notes before she spoke her mind.

We met in Lisbon later that month when she was going there to pick up an honorary degree for her services abroad. I could tell that Adelina was nervous and that was because she knew her mother was a straightforward person who would have called a sin by the name without going behind curtains.

"You said you did not want to get married when you were still young, after your father and I divorced," she said looking at Adelina.

We had talked about various things which happened in the past but she had never told me anything like that. She looked at me before she replied.

"Yes I did,." she said.

"What changed?"

"I was a young girl then who did not know whether I was ever going to be happy because of the things that happened to our family. Since I met Brooks things have never been the same again."

"So you have decided."

"I'm decided," she said, and then nodded her head to confirm it.

"Welcome to the family," her mother said extending her hand.

I rose up and took it. It was the same as that first day at Mark's when she was wishing me a nice stay at the Portuguese department.

"I warned you against moving too close to African men," she said, looking at Adelina.

She laughed.

"And you naughty boy who stole my daughter," she said pinching my cheek.

One year later, after a couple of meetings in Brasilia, we married in the local church at home where I attended my Sunday school when I was young. It was good to get married where Father Agostinho used to preach. It made me remember a lot of things. Meyer was right when he had talked about times and seasons for everything. To me and Adelina, it was different from the main events he had said. Death could have come then or the following day but I strongly felt that it was still far away. The only thing we cared about that that day was getting married and anything else would follow because we had made a vast stretch in life which we would have described as coming from far. My sister was the happiest person that day. She was glad that at last the ghost of loneliness was going away and the family was getting bigger.

After our honeymoon in South Africa, we decided to do a family reunion which brought us together. When we were moving to our new house, I took the framed words of Einstein from the walls and put it in our living room. I agreed with him that the best life a person could live was one that was dedicated to others, and I had made a decision that it was the beginning and not the end. There were several things that inspired us, whether living or dead. I was always appreciative and thankful to my mother, who, even in her absence, gave me energy to work hard and try to make meaning out of my life. Tracy renewed the desire of my service to other people even when I did not know whether there were Einstein's words on the wall of their living room like those which had existed on ours many years before. Faith was a symbol of care and kindness that never changed, even in the final steps towards her last breath.

We started our life when we moved to our house and there were a lot of challenges and expectations that waited for us. When we had our first child and it was a girl, I was thankful to the goodness and named her Uwimana after my mother, which in Rwandese meant 'daughter of God'. She would always remind me of her, even when I believed she was always behind everything I did. Russel took her in his arms when he came home from school and called her many pet names or sang her lullabies until she fell asleep. He was likely to take after his mother, who was the only person I knew who never got annoyed with me, even when I was young. I did not know then that the tender care in her was a genetic trait. They were the two sources of love which carried happiness in our marriage. I knew that there was no such a thing as living happily ever after. There were some families that broke up, but I had learnt one or two things from my family and that of Adelina.

It was ten minutes after six o'clock, almost the same time my mother died and one minute after my daughter was born. She did not have a first name. I decided to call her 'Minutes' so that she could always remind me about the time and become my diary. I stood in Adelina's botanical garden looking as far as the horizon where the setting sun had sunk leaving behind bright orange clouds. There were several buildings that had sprung up in the distance, which was a sign of life and development in the place that was once bushes and their shadows. The kids were playing around the house by chasing each other and pouring soil on each other's heads.

"That's okay," I said to myself.

I was glad that they were not lonely and took care so that they would not miss anything. I was determined to give them the kind of life I never had. I did not know what the following day would have brought, just like I did not know what was happening beyond the horizon even when I kept looking at it. It was a wonderful sight to look at and above all that was my home and my land where I belonged.

Even away from it, I could still hear the sounds of children playing in the ground of the children's home and I knew life existed because it was protected and valued. I could hear the newborns crying at the gulp of air in the delivery section of Agostinho Women and Children's Hospital. It was wonderful and that was the way life went on endlessly. I could hear the children crying in treatment rooms when they were receiving injections, and through such simple procedures better and healthy life was guaranteed. It did not matter at all if the children cried or laughed, as long as I knew that they were being taken care of. When we were around that place, Adelina spared time to go and play with the children. She would run along like a little girl while they chased her and I found myself laughing.

Adelina's voice came from the main house telling everyone that supper was ready and the table was set. It was good to hear her sound calling us to go and eat because it was soft and tender, which was a motherly thing. I felt my mother was always there because she used to do the same thing when food was ready. She would call me and tell me to bring my little sister in after which we would have a happy family meal.

"What did you cook?" Russel asked cheekily.

"Mashed potatoes and beef stew," she answered him.

"Nobody wants to bury dead things in his stomach," he shouted.

I laughed again. He had stuck to the joke after I told him the story about my grandfather who did not touch meat because he thought his stomach was not a grave to bury dead animals.

My small family was happy and I hoped that would continue. I did not know whether we would live to see rainbows forever, but I knew it was none of my business because time would have decided. The cotton white clouds were chasing each other in the sky and soon the area beyond the hill was going to be covered with darkness. That was okay. People needed to sleep and the only never-ending lullaby was that of nightfall. The flowers smelt sweet in the evening and they always reminded me of Adelina because she was the happiness of my life. I felt someone touch me from behind and without even turning I knew it was her. It was time for supper.

Glossary of Terms

1. *Favelas*-Portuguese word for slums

2. *Grota do surucucu-* Name of a slum in Brazil meaning 'hole of the surucucu.'

3. *Hiragana* and *Kanji-* A type of Japanese characters

4. *Rumba Portuguesa* –Refers to a type of music style created by Portuguese gypsies.

5. *Samba de gafieira-* A type of Brazilian Samba dance.

6. *cidade maravilhosa-* Portuguese words for marvelous city

7. clemência de Deus- Portuguese words for Mercy of God

8. "*Bom dia senhora Fabiano?*"Portuguese greeting which means 'good morning Mrs. Fabiano?'